SHATTERED

THOMAS CANNON

Tumbleweed Books
Tumble through the pages of our books

SHATTERED
THOMAS CANNON

Tumbleweed Books
Tumble through the pages of our books

Tumbleweed Books
HTTP://TUMBLEWEEDBOOKS.CA
An imprint of DAOwen Publications

Shattered / Thomas Cannon

ISBN 978-1-928094–79-1
EISBN 978-1-928094-80-7

Cover art by MMT Productions
Edited by Douglas Owen

10 9 8 7 6 5 4 3 2 1

To my wife, Linda, and my children, Kristen, Morgan, and Sawyer. They give me a warm, full life that inspires me to write that also includes two beautiful grandsons, Aiden and Callan.

1

Eagan Holiday Inn July 8th, 1995

A microphone runs out from the DJ booth. The gig is just a cocktail lounge and not a booking in a big comedy club. But it's a stage, and when I am done, I will want to go back up. It's my sanctuary.

I am six foot six and tower over the people sitting around the makeshift stage on the dance floor. My frizzy, long hair is hot from being too close to the light cans. Though I slouch on the stool, I still fill the stage. Besides being tall, I'm shaped like an all-star wrestler from the seventies or John Goodman. In other words, fat.

"I became a stand-up for the same reason as other comedians," I tell the people as they sip their drinks and gaze up at me. "To pick up women." The people laugh even though it's an old joke. Smoke from my cigarette swirls in the light. "That's what got all the great comedians into the business. Lenny Bruce. Richard Pryor. Jerry Seinfeld. Rosie O'Donnell."

This gets a bigger laugh than it deserves, but it's still a laugh.

"For eye candy like this one." I wink at a woman in the front row and mouth, "you and me, baby." With raised eyebrows, I thrust my pelvis at her a few times as if my crotch is a ping-pong paddle.

I shake her and her boyfriend's hand. "Only kidding." The other two comics have the crowd warmed up, and everyone has had enough to drink. Otherwise, no one would be laughing. I'm burned out from six months on the road.

The boyfriend has now put a protective arm around his woman. She is not beautiful but has a smooth, unblemished face with chestnut hair teased around it like a lion's mane. I like her eyes, and her laugh shows white teeth. There is always a woman like her in a low-cut dress showing off her tan scoops of cleavage. At least on Saturday night because it is date night. These sexy women always have a well-dressed husband or a boyfriend sitting next to them, but while I'm up here, their eyes are on me.

A guy is doing a lot of talking on my right, and every step I take clumps on the platform. Both are distractions, and I want to blame them for not getting into my rhythm. I've been off the whole night, though. It must be that Alaine is in the audience. I searched the crowd for my best friend from the kitchen doorway while waiting to be introduced. I'm searching for her now, and it is throwing my timing off.

"But dating is rough being this tall," I tell the crowd, gripping the mike stand. "On first dates, you always have to compliment the other person to break the ice, right? I always end up saying, You part your hair very evenly." I stand up and gaze down, pretending to check someone's part.

"The worst part is she usually returns with a" –I am now a short woman and squinting at a person towering over me– "nice nose hairs."

The crowd laughs. I let them, finishing my cigarette and finding the ashtray on the floor. A table of ladies is still laughing, so I give them more time by lighting a new cigarette and taking a drag. Smoking on stage is my prop, and it gives me my timing. I just have to avoid imitating Andrew Dice Clay.

"Speaking of being awkwardly big, I went shopping for clothes today," I say to them after a slightly too long lull.

I put the microphone close to my mouth. "Yeah, in the Jolly Green Giant's section. The only clothes I can find are bib overalls with Bubba stitched on the chest. Finally, I gave up and shopped at one of those big and tall shops. Naked and broke is what they should call them.

"All I could afford there was a pair of socks. No matter how thick that wool is, you need more than a twenty-dollar pair of stockings to survive a Minnesota winter."

I blow out smoke, making a cloud around my head. Too many people are looking at their bills.

"For some reason, people think they can make comments about my weight because I am tall. Things they wouldn't say if I was just fat, at least to my face. And it's not that they're not afraid I will beat them up, because they are, but because they think something so large must have less feelings.

"For example, before the show tonight, some woman asked if I was pregnant." They laugh.

"I told her, yeah, with an elephant. Want to see its trunk?"

Laughter.

I take a big drag. This is to take a beat because I haven't set up a transition to a new topic. "When I'm not doing stand-up, I'm an inventor to meet the needs of rednecks. My latest gadget is a lawnmower with an attachment for mowing under cars up on blocks."

Mild Laughter. Shit. Pity laughter.

I end with a big rant on growing up living with my mom and three sisters: all the while looking for Alaine.

"I'm Mikey Haskell. Thanks for being a great crowd." I put the mike on the stand and shake the emcee's hand. Even with a terrible set, I already want to go back up on stage and be in the moment and free. But being done brings me closer to being reunited with Alaine.

While the emcee closes the show, I pass his closing minutes by reading the signs posted on the bulletin board in the kitchen. After hearing a round of applause, I grab my coat from the back room and meander behind the crowd as it files out.

Alaine is standing down the hallway in tan pants and a corduroy jacket with her small purse hanging off her shoulder. She dashes toward me.

We haven't seen each other in months, and I'm shocked by how sophisticated Alaine looks. She doesn't look like a college girl anymore, but maybe it's just that she cut her long hair to jaw length.

"There you are," she says with a smirk. She hugs me and leans her slender body on me.

"Hi," I say and laugh.

"You were great tonight, Mikey."

I won't worry that she's lying about that right now. "Let's go feed that fat face of yours." I put my hand on her shoulder. My hand feels monstrous on her slender frame.

Phil Kearney, the featured comic of the night, strolls out of the lounge. "Mikey," he says, coming up to us. "We had the crowd the whole night. Wasn't it great?"

I smile. "You had them. I just had their carry-over mood."

"How much better was the sound system tonight? Last night, it was set up for music, the opposite of what it's supposed to be for voices."

"Didn't notice. Was it?"

"This your woman-friend?" He's almost leering at Alaine. I know he came over so he can get the low down on her petite body, blonde hair, and dark eyes under thin eyebrows.

"Well, she is a woman, and she is a friend."

"A close friend," Alaine says in a flirty way as she loops her arm around mine. "Very close," she adds so that for a moment, she can be a trophy in my display case. I'm not worthy of her, but at least I'm better than her real boyfriend, Dan.

"Good working with you tonight, Phil," I say, and Alaine waves to him as we head toward the door. Outside, I offer her a cigarette and put it to my mouth when she shakes her head.

I follow her to her apartment, where she drops her car off. Then she gets into the 1984 Honda Civic my parents loan me when I'm on tour. Even though she is my best friend, and we have ridden together a thousand times, my heart pounds to have her sit by me in the dark interior of the car. I get going without having discussed where because I don't know what to say. Alaine does. She knows how to reconnect with me. "Let's go to Perkin's like we always used to after bar time."

For the last six months, I have eaten alone or next to waitstaff folding napkins. Now I am following a hostess into a real restaurant with a pretty woman. It's like getting a pedicure after running a marathon in the desert.

We sit across from each other in a back booth, and my legs immediately feel cramped under the table. Our waitress stands with her pen in her hand and wordlessly waits until we order. I get a works omelet with sausage and a Coke, and Alaine gets what the menu calls a mammoth muffin. "Please make sure my muffin is mammoth," Alaine says to the waitress. "Last time, it was only humongous."

The waitress does not look up. "What to drink?"

The restaurant is filled with drunk people, and they are annoying. A big group has pulled tables together and is harassing the waitress. This is not what I wanted. Six months of being on the road changed things. I took any booking from the big clubs down to a high school lock-in. None of these gigs were even near the Twin Cities, but I can't let my disappearance change what Alaine and I have. We need a chance to talk like old times, and we cannot do that with all these drunks around. Too much has slipped away, though I called her from the road. We always had so much to say to each other. But the last few phone calls were filled with too much nothing and made me morose. I had nothing funny to say, so I didn't say anything. Alaine kept on talking to keep the silence from settling in. She talked about Dan, her friends, and her job.

I can't fault her for talking about those things, but it's just acquaintance talk. We needed to talk about important things like we used to do. "These people next to us won't shut up," I shout. "We should have gone someplace else."

"Wow. You're a little on edge there, Mikey. I thought you loved coming here to laugh at the drunk people."

"Err. They're morons." The people at the next table curse me.

Our food comes, and I stuff my mouth. "Mikey, are you seriously pissed off?" She touches my hand. "Think of it as payback for all the people we bothered when we came here drunk."

"Look at this stuff," I tell her in my comic voice, deciding not to get too quiet. I pull a strand of imaginary hair off my plate. "The most edible thing is the cook's hair."

"Shh," Alaine says, laughing at the same time. "Shh."

I like to make her squirm in public. Her laugh soothes my soul. In exaggerated movements, I eat my pretend hair like it was spaghetti. "Mmm. The cook's hair is prepared to perfection this evening."

"Mikey, stop. Before you make Miss Waitress from Hell come back." She glances over her shoulder. "Shit. She heard me." Alaine slides down in the booth and laughs. The waitress does come back over, and as Alaine hides from her, the waitress asks me in a noncommittal tone if she can get us anything else.

"Stomach pump, please."

"Hilarious," the waitress replies. She gives me a look that tells us my joke wasn't exactly original. "You oughtta be a comedian." I rub the whiskers on my chin and consider it as she leaves our bill and walks away.

Alaine doesn't notice when she sits back up that I am staring at her. She digs in her purse for the cigarettes she bought to smoke with me. I enjoy how her soft hair falls forward, so she has to tuck one side behind her ear and then the other. But her hair is too short to stay and cascades forward before she looks up. She finally glances at me with a tilted head. "What?"

Some women are good-looking, but their features are sketched on with broad strokes. The line of Alaine's brow, the soft nose, and the gentle lips around her small mouth all seem graceful, created with a fine brush. She's not dainty, though. Some women have to be treated with special care, and in return, they have nothing real to give. You can feel the conversation get lighter when they say something.

On the other hand, Alaine likes to laugh and have a good time, but I've never seen her be crude. Some women try to be like one of the boys. They wear baseball caps and belch as loud as they can.

"I don't know," I say after eating the last half of a sausage left on my plate. "Coming home put me in a weird mood. I stopped today while walking and watched two boys sitting on the steps to a house. They were about ten or eleven. By the looks of them, I thought they were troublemakers. That's what boys at that age want to be. But they were playing at some sort of pretending. I almost cried watching them. They weren't even cute kids. Maybe that's why I wanted to cry. But it was..."

"Moving." She smiles and touches my hand again. "I wish more people paid attention to things like that. Dan doesn't, that's for sure."

Walking away from the boys, the only thing I wanted to do was tell Alaine about them.

Alaine takes out another cigarette. She smokes with me; otherwise, she has given them up. "See, that's why I want all boys. Girls grow up too fast nowadays, but boys stay in a play world longer." She adjusts the ashtray. "Except for you, right? You were taking care of your sisters."

"I was a serious kid. My mom may as well have put me to work."

She flicks her ash. "My mom wanted me to be a tomboy. She wanted me to get out and do boy things, so I would grow up strong, but I was a total priss."

The restaurant has emptied by the time we leave. I pay because Alaine had to buy dinner many times when I was starting out. Alaine tucks a couple more dollars on top of my tip under our full ashtray.

"Making retribution with money?" I say. "We are probably the only Minnesotans willing to do that."

* * *

"Call me tomorrow," Alaine says when we pull up in front of her apartment building. Dan must be out of town because she would not have stayed out so late if he was home.

"I have to go to Duluth tomorrow and drop off the car."

She holds her purse in her hands. "Really? I thought your parents gave you this car."

"My step-dad doesn't give anything away. But it's fine. He wants to do the maintenance on it, and I want to get my car."

"You still have the old Beast? God, we took it everywhere in college. It must be a collector car by now."

"The market for a rusty '68 Ford is a little depressed right now." Lately, memories of college have been popping into my mind. Many of them include Alaine being the designated driver. It was a wonderful thing to have a girl drive your car. "With gas a buck fifteen, it doesn't make sense to keep it, but it holds so many memories."

"We need to go through my photo albums."

How about tonight? What the hell? Let's sit close and reminisce. Maybe we can go back to those old times. I want to say something to keep her from going but cower inside myself. It's as if I am sweeping others back with a torch. "Those times seem so long ago."

"Aren't you glad to be home, Mikey? Because I'm glad you're home."

I lay my arm across the steering wheel. "Being back in the twin cities has been a shock to my system. Larry booked me gigs close by to make me relax, but I don't remember how. The only thing I knew would recharge me is seeing you." I brighten up my voice. "So, nope. Not at all." She reaches over to hug me, and I jerk my arm in a panic to get it around her.

She opens her door. "Call me when you get back from Duluth. Are you going to watch me until I get in?"

"Of course. You ask me every time, and I always do."

"You know I'm nervous that there is some weirdo-"

"I know. I'll wait." She gets out of the car and goes through the security door. I wait until a light goes on in her apartment, then drive home on the backstreets. This is my second night home. I smoke two cigarettes on the drive to my apartment.

2

Old apartments that face north are gloomy. You can throw a lamp where dark surfaces suck up light, but that only reminds you that corners have you surrounded. Still, I turn on the ceiling lights in my dining room and the lamps in my living room. I even flip on the bug-filled fixture in my narrow aisle of a kitchen.

The only thing I wanted in the last six months was to see Alaine. It was great, but the stark contrast between her and here makes me regret coming home. I collapse on the couch so that tiredness does not get away from me, but my eyes refuse to close.

I flip to a rerun of Magnum P.I. Tom Selleck is the Barbie doll of the male image. It occurs to me to write that in the flattened spiral notebook on my coffee table. I haven't written anything in months and can't bring myself to do it now.

After a show is the best time to write jokes. When I am still wired from performing. Behind the couch is a filing cabinet of old journals. Instead of writing, I wait for a commercial to come on and rummage through the frig.

Hey, fatty, you just ate. I grab a bag of chips off the counter, anyway. As if to hide from my thought, I turn all the lights off and eat in the dark.

Magnum ends and infomercial after infomercial plays until I can't stand the TV anymore. It's getting lighter outside, close to a summer morning. I take off my clothes and lay down on my couch.

Sleep does not come.

I let the night with Alaine replay in my head until other thoughts intrude.

That's the cue to give up on sleep. Still naked, I go to my dining room and stand under the smoky glass light fixture. A cheap stand-alone mirror is the only thing in the room, and I have stood in front of it for countless hours to get the right expression for every joke.

My manager and other comedians tell me I have a great set. A few months ago, I would have agreed with them. But even though most of the audiences have not noticed, there is something stale about my act.

If Dan would've been home, Alaine would not have come to see me.

* * *

If someone burst in, I would cover my gut instead of my crotch. In this examination, I move onto my face because it is something I can't hide. My nose is too big, and I have fat under my chin. I look better with short hair (hey, I'm fat, but at least I groom), but I cannot remember my last haircut. My clean-cut appearance is gone, anyway. A few weeks ago, I left my toiletry bag at a motel.

I get my clothes on and come back to the mirror. It is my only hope of inspiring something better than crap about Tom Selleck. I made my success in front of this mirror. It does not reflect that back now. The loose-fitting T-shirt blurs my physique without hiding the size of my belly. I suck my gut in and let it sit naturally. I punch it to make it collapse in on like bread dough.

Fat jokes are in my routine, but I am uncomfortable with them and have to tell them boisterously. Even other fat comedians make me uncomfortable. All of their jokes are about being fat as if it is the most important thing about them. Fat is not who I am; it encapsulates me.

Think of a new joke. Just one. I open my notebook on the nearest surface, which is the stove just inside the kitchen. Phrases flip through my head like they are in a Rolodex, and I am thumbing through them. They are things that struck me as funny, but my mind rejects them. Instead, I think about how the lawnmower joke died. I've transferred it from notebook to notebook without ever getting it right. Then last night, I said it out of desperation.

Even when my set tanked and no one laughed, doing it made me high. I laughed at my own jokes like hack comedians that get the crowd going with their own laughter. Now I hate that joke, and the rest of them, for that matter.

At my request, Larry booked me all over the country. I wanted to be a road comedian. Hanging out at comedy clubs, going to empty matinees with other comedians, trying to find laundromats, and driving for long stretches called to me. Yes, even the mind-numbing activities. At the end, I hated it all.

Now I am home.

* * *

Things are not the same. I think it's because things are the same. Starting out, I enjoyed starting out. All my friends encouraged me to do open mikes at Pepito's in Minneapolis. I was terrible, but all eyes were on me. These formed my yearning for attention into something identifiable, like the vending machines at the Milwaukee Zoo that produce animals from hot plastic shot into molds.

Now standup is all I have.

I take boxes of textbooks and hand-me-down Christmas

decorations out of my closet and stuff the mirror in there. All my brain can think about is getting rid of it. The act holds the promise of sleep..

3

The sun is up between the two apartment complexes across the street. I am so tired it should not bother me. Yet, I keep track of the amount of sunlight through the patio door. The sun begins as a faint red through the clouds, but that gives way to bright sunshine. The new day is unbearable.

I get off the couch and make pancakes. The only other food is off-brand cans of tomato soup from Cub Foods that Mom brought me. There is no reason I would ever make soup. Drive-Thrus is why God made car windows that roll down.

Pancakes should drown in enough syrup that lifting a forkful should be like pulling a mastodon out of the La Brea Tar Pits. But I do not have any syrup and eat them dry. The only sound is my fork scraping the plate. Something in me is pleased my food is dry and tasteless.

That desire to suffer also wants to ignore the great time with Alaine last night and think about how she is going to marry Dan. They have been together for a long time, but he is not the right choice for her.

Some mistakes are mistakes, but some mistakes are fate.

Mine, for example. To ignore this troublesome fact, I go to my packed suitcase and transfer jeans, socks, and a T-shirt into my duffel bag. Then I change into a pair of jean shorts and a tank top also from my suitcase. Over the tank top, I put on a button-down shirt. The second shirt is a drape to help cover my fat.

* * *

I complete my look with aviators and a cigarette on my way to my car. If only I was somebody else, I would be cool.

It will be hot today. There was a fat guy in a lot of my classes, and he made jokes about how a muggy day should be an excused absence for anyone over 225 pounds. His excuse to sit and drink beer made me do things to show that was not true.

The Civic's air conditioning died a long time ago, so I'm used to driving with the windows open. It's the drive to Duluth I hate. 35E North is hell because it is summer, and people are going up from the twin cities to go to Canal Park to watch the aerial bridge. I understand that as I've seen the bridge rise to allow large cargo ships from Lake Superior to pass under. But it belongs to me. I am one of those that have to drive on it when the fog rolls in, and all you can see are the side rails and the cables reaching into grayness.

It is not long before the traffic and the heat get to me. I rub between my eyebrows and realize my whole body is tense from glaring out the windshield. The smart thing to do would be to pull over, but instead, I pop some No-Doze and wait for the only enjoyable part of the drive.

I pull over at the rest area on the crest of Thompson Hill. After enduring the reeking bathroom, I go to the overlook and take in Duluth and Superior, with the harbor between them and the lake beyond. We think we are hardy up here because of Lake Superior, but living in the sister cities is like living in any other small city in the Midwest. The special thing is to be up here and look out over the water, the cities, and the surrounding foliage.

The wooded areas are in firm control over the concrete whiteness of the buildings. Yet the roads lacerate them. I don't want to notice High Bridge and Highway 53 Bridge. They leave me with a mixture of disgust and awe the way they strap the bay down.

* * *

The lake spreads out to the horizon, and beyond it is the sky above. They are too big to comprehend. It's better to try, though, than to head down to my hometown and get mixed in with its humanity

My mom expects me, but I linger, looking at the city. The buildings and the factories with their smokestacks are oppressive, and the subdivisions keep pushing outward, but the ground and the trees put up a fight. Lake Superior stops human intrusion. If nature is worried, she doesn't show it.

All those lives going on down there. Each person believing their life is special. Some feel blessed by God. Some are sure they are cursed. People concentrate on what they have and what they do. Whether they are blessed or cursed, it is all indistinguishable up here.

From here, a good and a bad life look the same.

I force myself to go back to the car and drive down to intertwine myself for my little reason that I can take a nap.

The No-Doze has made me alert, but I cannot quite connect things. I confuse the layout of Duluth with some of the cities I work in regularly.

Grand Avenue is a street in Duluth. It's a street in every city. It's not until the neighborhoods become too familiar that I take the right streets to get to the low one and a half story house with a two-car garage set back from it. My childhood home is on a corner lot with a gravel driveway, so the first thing I see is my car parked beside the garage. The white four-door with rusted out wheel-wells, and dented driver-side door, waits for me.

The only thing different besides the amount of dust on my car is the portable basketball hoop. When I was young, my stepdad told me they were too expensive, and he did not want one attached to the garage because I would ding up the aluminum door.

* * *

Tammy, my half-sister, and my mother are watching a soap opera when I come in the back door. They both get up to meet me, with Tammy being first because she bounds into me. I try to return the intensity but am self-conscious because she has grown up in the seven months since I've seen her. I pry her away, so I am not pressed against her chest.

"Missed you, Squirt," I say, switching to my mom's hug. Her hug is passive, but that is how she is. "Hi, Mom."

"Oh, honey, you need a haircut and put on some weight." This is a typical greeting from my mom. "Do you need a snack?"

I shrug. I ate two cheeseburgers on the way up, but because she says snack, I need a snack.

Mom disappears into the kitchen while I plunk down on the couch and into my childhood. It's the same matching pictures of snowy woods with a row of deer racks arranged on the wall above my head. It's the same blue couch and the same brown recliner draped with an orange afghan. Mom and Chet have the same Curtis Mathes console TV, but it does have a new VCR sitting on top.

Tammy sits down in the recliner with one leg under her and lets the TV show catch her eye. "What are you watching?" I ask her because it's a commercial.

A man on the screen cuts a green bar of soap with a jackknife. "The Young and the Restless."

I smirk. "Shouldn't you be riding your bike or playing with dolls?"

"I'm fifteen," she says.

The soap opera fills the silence that follows. Coming home during college breaks felt no different than hanging out after a long day at high school. My sisters were happy to see me, and it was automatic that we would mess around in the backyard or play on my Sega.

"Carrie is at Jenna's house," Tammy says.

"I figured she'd be moved in there by now."

Tammy laughs. "Katie's at the pool."

"Wow. You guys are getting so grown up."

She rolls her eyes at me. "You sound like Grandma Betty."

Mom brings me a ham sandwich on a paper plate with a wicker plate holder. "Oh, damn it," she says. "I have to pick up Katie. Don't go traipsing around town until I get back."

"So wait to traipse until you get back. Got it. Only be here when you are not."

Officially alone with my sister, I wrack my brain to come up with something to talk about. She glances at me in a way that shows she is doing the same. It makes me dread the end of the soap opera.

I watched my sisters a lot. I loved it. Mom did not meet Chet until I was eight. Tammy was born a year later. At some point, my mom worked nights, and I became the main babysitter. Chet didn't get home until after six, and I was sure I was more of a father to them than Chet. Now, it feels like we are strangers. To have something to say, my tired brain comes up with a tease. "What's your boyfriend's name, Tam?"

"Jeremy," she says when I expected an eye roll. "He's coming over tonight." She flips to Montel Williams using a remote control for the tuner in the VCR.

"And has Mom and Chet met him yet?"

She looks at me. "Yeah. Dad had to meet him before we could go out on our first date. And we've been going out for five months."

Tammy's tone suggests she is irritated with me. I don't know why that would be. Though she wouldn't know, I am embarrassed that she has a boyfriend when I never had a date until out of high school. She might be having sex. If Tammy and this Jeremy have dry-humped once in the last six months, she has a better sex life than me.

Sad as that is, the old me could have made that into a joke.

Someone comes through the back door, so I call out to Mom. "See, I'm still here." But it's Chet in the doorway in his All Seasons Heating & Cooling uniform.

"Good for you, Mike," he says. "Tammy, where's Mom?"

"Getting Katie." She and I turn our attention to a loud commercial that comes on. Chet disappears. People are avoiding me, I think, even though Mom insists Chet change out of his work clothes.

The phone rings in the kitchen, and Tammy tosses the remote to me and runs to answer it. That leaves me alone with Montel and a kid trying to adopt his half-brother.

When the back door opens again, I head out to the kitchen. Katie leaps up into my arms. She is eight and asks me questions nonstop about how long I can be home and what cities I worked. Instead of waiting for me to answer her, she asks, "Did you go to Los Angeles? Did you go to Las Vegas? Did you go to Disney World?" Tammy sits on a step stool talking on the phone, and Chet and Mom are in the kitchen. I can hear Chet ask, "Wasn't he coming after dinner?" That doesn't feel good to hear, but I'm listening for the need to defend Mom from one of Chet's rants.

Mom questions Chet about why he is home so early. While I try to get Katie to loosen her grip around my neck, Mom keeps asking questions. She wants to know why he didn't tell her he was taking time off. He waits for her to stop talking and tells her he wants to get some things done around the house.

It all overwhelms me, and I can't focus on anything. Katie is small for her age, but she gets heavy. I lean over so that she has no choice but to let go. My own increasing irritability drives me to the couch, but Katie follows and snuggles up next to me.

"I tell everyone my brother is a stand-up comic," Katie says. "Everyone thinks that's so cool."

I manage a smile for her. As a baby, she loved sitting in my lap as I rubbed her soft cheeks across my face. In my exhaustion, I can only see how much she looks like Chet.

All the girls do. Katie has a round face with freckles across her nose like Chet and fine hair. She even has his blue eyes. Carrie is the thirteen-year-old version of Katie.

Tammy has dark eyes and dark thick hair like my mother's. Still, you can tell that she is Chet's daughter. Up until now, at this moment, all I see in my sisters is my love for them.

"Do you have the keys to the Honda?" I slowly pick out that Chet is asking me this. My sisters and I used to be so close. "The keys, Mike."

The keys are in my pants pocket. "Katie, I got to get up." She takes this as a game and clings to my neck. "Come on, Katie."

"Nope. Stay right here."

I take a step and let her hang off my neck. Chet crosses his arms.

"Come on, Katie."

Mom steps in and tells her to get down.

Chet takes the keys and heads out to the garage. I take long strides to pass him to clean the car out before he does anything. As Chet stands behind me, I grab the fast-food wrappers and empty soda cups and jam them into a Burger King bag. "I clean it out all the time. It gives me something to do for a movement break on the road."

"Looks like it."

"Well, not in a while." Obviously. I take out my cassette case with tapes of my routines I used to critique myself and my checkbook stuffed with a bunch of bills to pay. Then I grab the pack of cigarettes off the dash. Chet, after watching me, goes to his garage.

I squeegee the change on the center console into my open hand and dump it into my pocket. There's more to get thrown away or put into my car. The full ashtray gets dumped into the Burger King bag from under the seat. I remove the maps from my glove box and both side pockets of the front doors. From the trunk, I get my toolbox and jumper cables.

"You're getting the car back," Chet says to me as I go back to the trunk and pocket the ring box with jittery fingers. "I'll have the maintenance done before you leave."

"Sometimes it's good to get everything cleared out." I light a cigarette that has found its way to my mouth.

Chet comes over and surveys the empty trunk before shutting the lid. Chet is shorter than me, and through Chet's eyes, I see me. I see my dad. And even as I make a suggestion that has been obvious for the last year and a half, I realize it's a threat to Chet's territory. "Plenty of places in the cities can do anything the Honda needs."

"No," he says. "It's my car. I will do the maintenance." He takes the keys off the roof where they've been sitting since I opened the trunk and gets in.

He starts it. Listens. I know what comes next, so I confess, "The muffler split open in Des Moines."

"You went to someplace like Midas, didn't you?" I shrug. "Of course, you did. It's just like you to put something on my car that is going to rust right out. What else did they scam you into getting?"

They wanted me to change the brake fluid, but I only said yes to new wipers and a blinker light. Before I can tell him this and that the muffler has a lifetime guarantee, he winds the car onto the lawn and backs into the garage. This is why I wanted to stay on Thompson Hill. Here Chet is getting me caught up in some muffler dilemma.

But I have put myself in this meaningless drama as well. I can afford a fuel-efficient car of my own. It is only my superstitions that stop me. The Honda is my greasy good luck charm that made me a successful feature comic all over the country. Just as my old Ford helped me go to gigs around the twin cities. Though it cost more in gas than the gig paid, it never failed to get me to a club.

The front door of my car creaks as I climb into its roomy driver's seat. In college, my friends named the four-door Galaxy 500 "The Beast." I pump the gas pedal until my leg aches before turning the key. Still, it sounds like the engine is not going to start.

Then the engine fires off, and a cloud of blue smoke billows out. I rev it so it will stay running. Then I rev it again and drop it in gear to get away from Chet. It wants to die as it breaks out of the ruts it sunk into.

When the ruts release it, the car flies down the driveway, and I have to lay on the brakes.

Tammy watches me from the side of the house. I roll down the passenger window to talk to her. Instead, she gets in.

"I've been waiting for a ride in The Beast," she says. "Jeremy wants to buy it from you so he can make it into a hot rod."

"So, he's a motor-head, huh?"

She laughs. "No."

We roll into the street, and I give it gas. Not too much, though, as the hood of the car spreads out in front of me like the deck of a destroyer. I am so used to the sloping hood of the Honda I worry we will side-swipe a parked car.

A few houses past ours is a small park with the same metal playground equipment my sisters and I played on. For a moment, I can see my sisters on the wobbly merry-go-round and me at twelve pushing them. This memory is more real to me than being in the car with Tammy, who has a boyfriend who thinks he knows about cars but doesn't hurt his ego by making fun of it. Or perhaps she makes fun of it, and he knows enough to not get mad.

I tromp on the gas to hear the V-8 rumble. "Well, this car is not for some punk to beat on."

"He's not a punk, Mikey."

"I only meant this is my car. All my high school experiences were in it. Well... not really experiences. They were more like incidents with misfits." I am no longer talking to Tammy but performing. It's not the right thing to do right now, but it relaxes me.

"I liked your friends."

We haven't seen each other in a long time. I preferred my college friends. Turning onto Superior Street to go through downtown, I try to think of something interesting to show Tammy. Nothing will compare to the real social life she has. "Perhaps I should get rid of the old Beast. It's not like we were sitting on the hood drinking beer at the quarry. It was four geeks cruising around in a rusty car. The closest we got to talking to a girl was ordering food in the drive-thru, and they were probably laughing at us."

"Mikey, I–"

"Not that I want to forget those guys. But I never call them up because they don't want to remember high school either. We got picked on a lot."

"Mom and Dad didn't know."

The best thing to do right now is to go take a nap. My sister doesn't want to hear what I'm about to say. "I was called every fat name in the book. Everyone hit me, too. I could take a hit without flinching, so then everyone was taking punches to get me to flinch. They half-thought I was in on the fun.

"When I got this car, it did not make me popular. But it was mine, and it meant escape." Tammy is looking at me. "So? How's high school going for you?"

Tammy is about to say something. I stop her. "Find out from that punk how much he was thinking."

We drive by Alaine's parents' house, a yellow ranch on a crowded street, and slow down as if they'd be waving from the porch. "Their initial response to me was fear like their daughter brought home a bear to eat them." I laugh at that pain. "Alaine and I only met through the rideshare board at college. But once they got to know me, they always invited me over when we were home from college." Alaine's endorsement of me brought them around, but I'm not sure she knows me at all.

"You liked college, right?"

"God, I was everything I wasn't in high school. In other words, happy. Are you thinking about college already? It must seem–"

"Mikey." Her tone is something only a fifteen-year-old can pull off. It says I don't know anything, yet I can help you. She wants to say something to make me feel better about breaking up with Karen. It's why she went on this ride with me.

I get a memory that lands in my mind often. We are at the dinner table. It feels like a holiday meal, and Tammy has a little child's voice. She asks Mom if I am her real brother. Even at the time, I knew she was trying to make sense of what a stepfamily is, but her question stays with me.

"I'm always here for you," she says.

What she should be is a little girl I can take care of. Not a teenager with a boyfriend and pity for me. "I know that, Silly."

In the driveway, Tammy gets out while I sit for a few moments, searching my mind for places we missed on the drive. Half my friends live in the twin cities now. I could go back and see Alaine's parents, but this ain't college. I could go to Arby's, where I worked in high school, but if any of my old crew is left, we'd only rehash old stories. Arby's leads me to contemplate a drive-by my ex-girlfriend's house. She was my first girlfriend, and we got together the summer out of high school. I did enough slow driving past her parent's house after she dumped me, and she is married with two kids now. Each scenario ends up with me regretting leaving the driveway.

"Mikey?" Tammy says, peering through my window.

"All roads lead to the same dead-end."

"Ha. Ha. Stop being weird. Supper is on the table."

"Yeah. I wanted to sit here for a moment."

"It's been like twenty minutes."

"No. Not that long." I take my keys out of the ignition.

"What were you thinking about, Mikey?" Tammy asks, not my little sister, but a teenage stranger. Maybe we can get re-acquainted when I'm older.

"Nothing. That's what people do once they are no longer a kid. They sit around and space out. Which is good because that's the only thing to do in a hotel by yourself." Well, there is one other thing.

Tammy comes closer to me. It's so she can lean on the door, but it makes me uncomfortable. "You looked like you did as a kid. You were always so serious."

I move and bang my knee on the steering column. "Ouch. I thought I was a fun big brother."

"You were. Totally," she tells me in a sweet voice. She can tell that I am upset. "But also, so dutiful."

I nod to end the conversation and pull the door handle.

4

Chet is at the table, now in his T-shirt. Taking off anything too grease-smudged is his version of dressing for dinner. Mom brings in lasagna, my favorite. She mentions it might be a little dried out from warming in the oven.

"How's the lasagna?" Mom asks me as I bring the first forkful to my mouth.

I chew but feel a time constraint to answer before swallowing. "Fine," I answer, looking around at my sisters, but Mom has only asked me. The truth is it tastes bland. Perhaps your taste buds stop working when you are exhausted.

Why aren't my sisters talking? I need them to ask me how I'm doing and to answer them that everything's fine. I've been MIA for six months, and that warrants some attention on me. Not pity, but questions that will lead to me making a joke.

"When are you going to need the car?" Chet is talking to me again. "It needs a new timing belt."

"I'll just buy a new car." I regret that it comes out like that. "There's no point in putting money into something so old just for me to run it down."

Mom tells me, "Chet got that car for you to drive and take to your gigs."

He got that car to control me. I'm too tired to argue about something so meaningless. "I'm thankful. But now it's a hassle."

"Well, you are not driving your car."

I glare at Mom. "I have a good down payment for a new one. A car with an automatic transmission and air-conditioning."

"You have shows this year," she answers. "What about next year if they dry up? You need savings."

"That Honda is your best option. Great gas mileage. By the way, I have it mechanically sound." Chet stands up and walks to the back door. "Ungrateful son of a bitch."

"What's up his ass?" I've never responded to Chet swearing at me before. "I said I was thankful, but it has to happen sooner or later."

"Don't swear in front of the girls." Mom picks up her silverware and her plate with food on it. "Supplying that car is how he shows he cares about you. He's been more than a father than your real dad ever was."

"You forced him into it." I stand up. "You've been forcing me on him since you met him." All the times I fantasized about blowing up over this subject, I thought I'd be giving it to Chet. Not Mom. There's no denying this new revelation to myself, though. "You forced Chet to feel something toward me that he didn't."

The girls are looking at me, but I'm too weary to pretend. "All this pretending has wearied me. Each time you pressed me on him, you made him reject me. You didn't let him just do what he could."

"He did enough."

"Goddamn it. You forced me on him. You nagged at him to be my dad a thousand times. The answer on his face was always no. Not I won't, but I can't."

"Don't talk about Chet that way in front of your sisters."

"It's not him. It's not his fault." I stand up, towering over the table and my sisters. The meal is so far down below me, but my mom seems to be meeting my gaze at eye level. "You were trying to pawn me off. You didn't want me either."

A new memory hits me. Perhaps it's not real. My father gets into a battered truck and drives away while we stand and watch, my mom's hand on my shoulder.

"You are not acting like yourself." She stacks up dishes off the table and carries them into the kitchen. I become smaller as she goes through the doorway. How many times did she disappear into the kitchen and leave out the back door? Grandma would snuggle me aggressively on the couch to distract me. I always knew she was leaving to go on a date.

"I didn't need a dad. Just like the girls don't." I meant my sisters are like daughters to me, but they don't need me anymore. I want to explain, but my mom stands with her back to me. Her fists are clenched to the side of the countertop. She will not turn around until she can be strong.

"How can you say that about Chet?" Her words are measured, divided up like pats of butter.

"I'm sorry I was a burden on you," I say. "Even though sorry is not good enough." I pick up my overnight bag by the back steps and walk out.

Chet has the garage door open and a country-western station on the clock radio. It is still bright out but cooler with the wind off the lake. Leaving on a bad note will require a long conversation later. This means that even as I walk to my car, I am still trapped. Unless I stay away. The idea of sneaking into the basement to get a storage bin of fall clothes sends me back toward the house. Chet meets me outside the garage.

"Do me a favor," he says. "Come back in a couple of days for the car."

"I told you–"

"For no other reason than it's an excuse to come back and visit your mother and your sisters. And me."

What he has just said is a message. He delineated everyone in the family without including me. Well, please exclude yourself.

"You haven't been around much since you got up with that Minneapolis girl." That girl who is nothing more than a city to him was everything to me. "So, come back in a few days."

That is not happening. "Thanks, Chet. Tell Mom we had a nice talk, so she thinks everything is smoothed over."

"Real good," he says.

I get into the car and back out of the driveway before Mom comes out. Still, I fumble to get a cigarette going before putting the car into drive. Everybody is hurt by what I said. My words are foggy in my mind, but I don't want to take them back.

5

The drive back to the cities seems to take forever. Each exit beckons me to pull over and close my eyes. When I finally do, I am too agitated to sleep. At Del Rancho Better Off Without Mikey, Mom has the dishes done and is watching TV while a pink boom box plays in one of the girls' rooms. Chet will come in from the garage, and things will be back to normal.

* * *

As soon as my eyes open, I turn the dome light on and check my watch. It's almost ten p.m. Lights are on in Alaine's apartment, but I am too groggy to go talk to her. To avoid dwelling on the three hours taken from me by sleeping in my car, I drive to Humphrey's Humor house, one of the four comedy clubs in the Twin Cities.

I walk through the lobby area with framed, signed pictures of comedians that performed here. The stale, ancient air and the rough brick walls are comforting. The old black and white tiled floor gives over to carpeting in the seating area. It's slow tonight. Behind the audience of twelve are rows of empty tables. A sixtyish guy (thin, with a full head of silver hair like the Marlboro man) stands at the mike with a drink in his hand. He goes to all the open mikes. His delivery and stage presence is great, but his jokes are old and stolen. George Burns shuffling on and off the stage was my idea of perfect golden years. But seeing an older man in front of a small crowd makes me want to quit comedy immediately.

I go to the back room off the main seating area. It's for rehearsal dinners or small reception, but just inside is a big corner booth where the comics hang out for their time slot. Dave is there with two other comics, but the number of empty glasses, bottles, and full ashtrays suggest there used to be more guys here.

"Mikey," Dave calls out with a grin that tells me that his set went well, and he has had several drinks since then. I don't know the other two comics but give them a nod. One of them grabs his jacket to go pay his tab, which means the club will close soon. The other must have the last time slot because he gets up to go to the green room. Waiting to go on and then walking through the audience to go up on stage sounds like torture to me tonight. Still, there is an old stand-up superstition that you lose it if you don't do it, and I think about finding Bill, the manager, and going on.

But I sit down and snag one of the ashtrays while Dave finds his bottle of beer in the debris of the table. Dave and I met at an open mike two years ago. He teaches English at Highland Park Senior High and does spots around the cities as a hobby. Perhaps it will become more than a hobby, but he is the basis of my joke about being a stand-up just to meet women. He almost told me he was in it for the tail in the same breath as telling me his name.

"It's about time you came down here," he says. "I had to keep busy by drinking in your absence." Dave is fifty-one but looks a lot younger with a dimpled chin, and his short, thinning hair jelled straight up on top. He has on a black T-shirt and a pair of expensive jeans. Even when he dresses down, he is more dapper than me.

"I've done three things since getting back. After my set last night, I spent time with Alaine, saw my family, and now I'm here with you."

He laughs. "As long as I'm in the top three. It's been a long time since you've been around."

I squish myself into the booth like trying to push crescent roll dough back into its pop-open canister. "Yeah, my career is supposedly going very well."

"Don't play that modesty shit with me. You're kicking ass and taking names. Everyone knows you're playing the big clubs on the coast." He spreads his arms out on the back of the booth. Then he smirks. "How'd the Holiday Inn go last night? They let you use the pool?"

"It came and went," I laugh at his nicely set up jab. My depression is gone now, as it only wants to attack me. Or maybe I am just relieved to be talking about the business. "How about you? How'd they treat you tonight?"

A waitress comes back by us, and Dave gets another beer and one for me. Dave finds two full shot glasses from somewhere on the table and slides one my way. We snap our heads back at the same time to down the alcohol. "The crowd was bigger, maybe thirty people. I didn't bomb, but it's hard to create any connection to the crowd when they are sitting at those round tables. Of course, comedians will find anything to blame for a terrible set. The crowd, the sound system, the candle centerpieces."

I light a cigarette. "This place won't last much longer. And once the last real club closes here, you'll have to go on tour."

"This place will close, but Acme will stay. And Lou will certainly make money with Knuckleheads, and I'll go there, even if it means going into the Mall of America." He shakes his head. "No. There is too much downtime on the road."

I stretch my arm across the top of the booth. "Most of it, you're driving. And by the time you unpack and check out the porn on the in-house channel at the hotel, it's time to go down to the club. I kept busy enough."

He shakes his head again. "You should have experienced stand-up here in the eighties. Comedy clubs popped up like zits on a teenager. It was the golden age for stand up in the cities."

"It sure ain't that way now," I say. Dave talks about this all the time, but I want him to go on. We both love the history of stand-up in Minnesota.

"I did think all the clubs were going to close." He takes a drink. "Some will tell you it was cable that killed the industry around here. That people could watch stand-up on TV for free. But it was all the bad comics that got stage time. Now, at least the kids that are making it, like you, are making it because you have talent."

I take a drink of my beer because I can't say anything. It means a lot that Dave would say that. Even though I can't believe it.

He stares at me. "So, then, how long are you home?"

"A good while. The local circuit likes the exposure I've been getting, so Larry set me up with gigs close by. And then he is making me take a little vacation." The waitress comes to check on us, and Dave gives her a little wink.

The booth is positioned so I can see the stage in the main room out of the corner of my eye. The comic that went to the green room is now on stage and sits on a stool with his feet on the rungs. Behind him is the plastic lit Humphrey's sign and a cream-colored brick wall. I would not be able to go on stage tonight. What about my set tomorrow?

"I'm glad you're home, Mikey," Dave says to me, bouncing a cigarette in his mouth as he speaks. Then he lights the cigarette. The waitress brings us two more beers and two more shots. "I know you were out on the road working, but you didn't come back at all."

"I worked everything Larry gave me. Doing what it takes to make it big."

"But you didn't even swing by."

"Larry didn't give me the time." A lie. I take a drink of beer. "And in fact, I should probably take off. I'm not feeling too well."

"Yeah, you really don't look so good. Are you okay?"

"Tired. I'll be better in the morning." I pick my cigs and lighter off the table.

"Okay. But we need to catch up. Are you doing anything with Alaine and Dan after your show tomorrow?"

"Dan is out of town. But Alaine is my friend, not Dan, anyway." I notice that the last comic's voice has stopped coming through the sound system. It has been replaced by the tinkling of glasses as the waitresses clear the tables.

"You don't have to explain things to me, man. I'd be trying everything to dip my stinger in her honey."

This comment corrals me into staying in the booth. "Christ, Dave, it's not like that." That has become a lie over the last few months. I don't want to admit it to myself, but my feelings have changed toward her.

"Easy, big guy. It was a joke. But come on, you can't tell me you wouldn't butter her biscuit if the opportunity presented itself."

I shrug my shoulders, but my face gets hot and gives away my feelings. "Yeah, she's beautiful. But she's the best person I know, too. She's very giving, very real. She would do anything for anybody."

"Then get her fiancé out of the picture, so you got a shot. Brainwash her or something." Dave looks at me. "Seriously. Put the moves on her. I wouldn't trick her. But I'd test the waters and see if I couldn't climb up on her naked." He stares at me. "Sorry. I get graphic when drunk, but–"

"You say whatever comes into your head, don't you?"

He downs his second shot. "It's easier than thinking."

"But..." I hesitate, surprised at what I almost say, though it's tame compared to what Dave is suggesting. "I have been thinking about something a lot lately. It was right before they got engaged. Dan was traveling all the time with his job, and when he was home, he spent a lot of time going out, so she kicked him out of their apartment." I drink my shot and some beer. "I was there for her, and I really think, now, looking back on it, that she had romantic feelings for me. But I was too stupid to realize it, and at the time, I was in love with my girlfriend." I see another full shot on the table and down it. "Then Dan made this grand gesture of re-arranging his job, so he'd be home more, and they got back together."

"So now, you're free, and she's tied down."

"But it's like he trapped her. He's back to being on the road all the time, and I think she's getting married just because she has her dress bought. She wouldn't be the first to make that mistake." My voice gets hoarse. I need to shut up. But I have a lot to sort out. "We spent a night together. Not like you're thinking, we talked. We were always close, but that night we held each other." I am getting into subjects men don't talk about and disconnect from it because I am going to keep going. "But isn't that what everything is about? To get as close to another human being as you can."

Dave throws his arms out toward me. "Just what I said. Seduce her."

"I don't want to trick her. I want my chance with her back. It would make the last year not have happened."

He looks at me, puzzled. "Absolutely. So should I come for your set tomorrow, or are you going to beguile Alaine?" The waitress comes with his tab, and he hands her a credit card.

"We'll probably do something before the show. But don't come. It's not worth it. It's not like my routine has changed."

"I'm there for the chicks, Mikey. You professional comedians get all the tail. I just want your throw-offs."

"Not me. Everyone else does, though."

"You're kidding me," he says. "Women come on to me all the time, and I'm only doing open mikes."

Women love comics, and other guys have women throw themselves at them. But after the shows on the road, I'd only go to a bar with the waitstaff or pick up food to take back to the club's condo with the other comics. Which was still better than going back to my empty apartment.

The waitress comes back with a receipt to sign and stacks glasses to carry to the kitchen, a clear sign it's time for us to go. In case we miss it, she gives us a get-the-hell-out-of-here look when she wipes the table with a wet rag. Dave gives her a little wink.

"You don't take them up on it, do you?" I ask.

"No," he says. But he does.

6

I am out for a walk after only a few hours of sleep. My head is feverish like the flu, but I am determined to lose weight. The same mind that tells me gas station fruit pies are still fruit tells me to jog, but I don't want someone to laugh at the sight of me and make me their joke. This huge, fat guy was jogging today, and there wasn't even a Dunkin' Doughnuts in sight. Besides, by walking, I can smoke.

The weather is right for smoking. The air is wet with mist, and the temperature dropped overnight. As if I am a lonely character on a movie set, I walk down the street with a cigarette in my mouth and my hands in my pockets. The mist wets my clothes and hair.

I throw the cigarette away and pick up the pace to get some actual exercise out of this. But more than that, I am trying to get away from being home, making me maudlin, and the weather is not helping.

This is my homecoming. Why doesn't Alaine miss me in a commensurate amount to how long I was gone?

Why were things easier on the road? Because I did not have to face that everything good has gone away. My friends are gone or still in the cities, but we have lost touch. When I abandoned my high school friends during college, I identified that you outgrow friends. But that is not what is happening now. I am sinking away from people. I am a little boy in my bedroom listening to laughter from the living room.

A girl that is about ten is out in the rain just to wear the yellow raincoat she has on. She is walking with one foot on the curb and the other on the sidewalk. Up. Down. Up. Down. Her mass of auburn hair in pigtails is bobbing around. Her cheeks are red from the cool air. I slow my lumber and watch her come toward me. I am struck by this lonely picture. No one should walk alone.

Children make me smile. If I had a daughter like this little girl, we could walk in the rain together. A son like the boys on the steps would be wonderful as well. That's the real reason they caught my eye.

There are sad things in this world, and I am one of them. Even the beautiful things, such as the red-faced girl who is now swinging around a light pole, are in danger of being swallowed up. My throat tightens as she runs to the steps of her house.

At first, I wanted a friend for her or a group of friends to splash in the puddles with. Somehow, I felt guilty for her being alone. But she is fine. There will be warmth inside to draw out the color in her cheeks. She has people waiting for her. Still, in my mind, the beauty of the little girl mixes with the pain of her being solitary. Solitary is a game played by ugly people at the kitchen table.

My legs turn to stone, but I go on with my walk.

7

Alaine opens cabinets as she talks to me on the phone. It is quarter after six, and the sounds of her making dinner tell me Dan gets home tonight, and she wants to be home for him. Otherwise, she would have called me earlier so we could meet for dinner.

I am only good enough when Alaine has nothing better to do.

It wasn't always that way, so I accept it, but I'm not in the mood to be her entertainment today. After talking to her for a few minutes, I say, "This is Mikey's answering machine. He's not here right now, so leave a message after the beep." I beep.

She says, "Funny, Mike. Anyway-" I hang up.

I stare at the phone, knowing she will call back. When she does, I have to feel better. I have to go on. "Oh, are you there now?" she says. "I called earlier. Did you get my message?"

She gets a laugh from me for extending the joke.

"Mikey, that reminds me of how we used to call people at three in the morning," she goes on. I was the one who made the calls. "We leafed through the campus phone book. Did they list the students' hometowns? They must have. We would call people at random and ask for a ride to their hometown, you know, like we were from there, too."

"Some of those people talked to me for twenty minutes before they realized I was bullshitting them."

Alaine continues about things we used to do. She talks about our freshman year when a group of five or six of us found this playground near campus late at night. It was the same group we did everything with. Mostly it was Alaine, Karen (before she was my girlfriend and just Alaine's friend), and me who spun around on the merry-go-round and swung on the swings. The others drank and smoked at a picnic table. They were those rare experiences that are beautiful, and you know it. The sky was cloudless, the crickets were singing in the tall grass along the fence, and we had just enough to drink to feel giddy. I remember pushing them on the merry-go-round, their hair flying out behind them as they passed me and smiled.

Alaine and I returned to the park once after Karen left for graduate school. She couldn't have looked more beautiful or natural on the equipment, but I felt ridiculous.

I am quiet as she talks. She even leaves herself open for me to make a joke. She does it on purpose, but I do not take the jab. This is childish, like hanging up on her before. I know I am just trying to get her to ask what is wrong with me, but I do it anyway.

"Mike, I've been meaning to ask you," she says. "Do you have a girl these days?"

This is as close as she will get to asking me if I am all right. It shows she cares, but it's not good enough anymore. Close the door. "Now, what do I need with one of those?"

"You don't. We are all a bunch of bitches."

I light a cigarette. The flu I'm getting makes it taste terrible. "Every one of them," I say. This will hurt her.

"Mikey, I tried to talk to you after you left. But you wouldn't come home, and you wouldn't ever be serious on the phone."

"I'm being serious now." I can't stop myself from saying this. "The only woman I love is you. Of course."

"So, that's a no to the girlfriend, then?"

"You know why, don't ya?"

She must know I am setting up a joke because she uses a great straight-man voice. "No, Mikey. Why?"

"By choice, sweetheart." After a couple of seconds, I hang up.

I snuff out my mostly unsmoked cigarette. After lighting another one, I dress for my set- a pair of Levi's, a gray T-shirt, and a button-down jean shirt. Then I replace the cigarette with a third. With this one, I make myself a new attitude for the show with each puff.

My lack of shaving is another asinine ploy. Looking in the mirror has been a challenge, but I want someone to notice I am sick and tired.

As I let The Beast idle and warm up, I choke down four gas station aspirins for my achy joints. The nostalgia of driving my old car to a gig makes me decide to do some of my early jokes. Normally the city and the crowd determine which jokes to tell and in which order. I have no plan tonight other than to bring back these long-retired bits. The audience can laugh if they want. They can do whatever they want. I pull out and try to remember the best way to 35E South.

* * *

The stage is too high tonight. The audience and I are on different floors of a house. That's how high. Although I had the chills before being introduced, it is too hot on the stage. Like many nightclubs in the metro area, Hotshots is part of a bowling alley. To get to the bar, you pass through an open field of bowling lanes. The bar's entrance is through two sets of large double doors that lead into a loud, dark place with a dance floor and a DJ; this Saturday night, the stage takes up the dance floor. It's a pretty good crowd, but there are more people here to bowl than to hear comedy.

"Who came up with the idea for a weatherman to show maps and talk about high and low systems?" I ask this crowd. "If I was interested in that shit, I would have become a meteorologist. Just tell me if it is going to rain or snow. Do we need to wear long johns, or is it going to be call-in-sick-to-work cold?" They laugh. It seems to be a crowd that laughed more because I said shit than the joke. But I can't tell tonight with me being so far above them. "That is what we need to know."

"And what is with calling off school these days when there is a half-inch of snow on the roads. In my day, when it snowed, they stood a kindergartener outside the door and didn't call off school until the snow was up to his neck."

"Another thing that bugs me is four-year-old kids wearing Nikes." I focus on the space just above the audience. "Nike high tops! On a baby! The boy is three feet tall. How are his shoes going to make him slam-dunk?" I jump spastically, pretending to be four years old and holding a basketball. My feet make a large banging sound as I land, and the risers shake enough to scare me. Still, I keep jumping and landing with big thuds. Then I look way up as if there is a basketball hoop over my head. "Ah, screw it," I say, throwing my imaginary basketball down. "I'm going to go play in dog poop."

The crowd stops laughing too quickly. I turn and go to the edge of the stage and peer down at the people in the front row. "That is why kids do not need fifty-dollar Nikes. They play in poop. They should go barefoot. Feet are wash and wear."

The room spins, and I grab the stool to sit down. I shouldn't have jumped around on the stage feeling so feverish. In this unintentional pause, the crack of pool balls and the synthesized speech of a pinball machine intrude. The stage is set up in the middle of this wide but not deep nightclub running the length of 50 lanes. On my left is the bar, black and chrome, and on my right are the pool tables and video games. I have been competing against these sounds all night, and I am ready to give up and tell these people to go bowl a couple of frames and come back for the headliner.

Silence has gone on too long, so I say something. "But I want to have kids someday. And I will as soon as I can get a woman drunk enough." The crowd laughs at this old, stupid joke. "Actually, a few sober women were willing to date me. I can get girlfriends, but they keep dumping me like garbage off a cruise ship." the crowd gives me a quiet, supportive laugh.

"My first girlfriend right out of high school called me a lifesaver. She said because of me, she found the strength to break up with her old boyfriend, who was this totally abusive, drunk loser." The crowd is quiet. Even the guys playing pool have stopped. Why am I getting into this? My act is turning, but I can't stop it. It is already in motion. The audience senses the shift away from the rehearsed, funny monologue they have come here to listen. But for the moment, they are still with me.

"After eleven months of going out with me, she found the inner strength to go back to him. If I was Luke Skywalker, Princess Leia would have married Darth Vader." It gets a laugh—a good, quick one.

"I rebounded fast, though. Two short years later, and I was dating again." I pause for a laugh from the audience. They don't give me one, so I make a funny face to punctuate my statement, my true statement. I think they only see the panic on my face. But I smile my practiced smile. "This girl was studying to be a veterinarian. That's how we met. I had a sore throat, so I had the choice of getting some Band-Aids and penicillin from the clinic on campus or going over to the School of Veterinary Medicine.

"Actually, that was the only clinic that had a scale that could weigh me. I had to wait in line at the scale while they weighed a moose." The crowd laughs.

"Okay, I went there as a gag. I thought the veterinary students would get a kick out of it, but it turns out I had a lot in common with their other patients." I imitate a gorilla. The crowd laughs at my silliness, but it is to release some intensity of what I am telling them and how I am telling it to them. This needs to stop being confession and return to a comedy act. That girl in Duluth did break up with me to go back to that guy. She preferred a jerk over me. And I did go to the vet clinic as a joke. It was the only gesture I could think of to show

Karen we should be more than friends. If it didn't work, I could play it off as a prank.

But I need to act like this is a bit. I pace on the stage in a Groucho Marx-like stomp. Being home is ruining me. I can't get away from my feelings.

"Then. Then I ended up getting engaged to the girl from the vet clinic," I tell the crowd, still pacing. "Engaged, serious, you know. Let's spend the rest of our lives together kind of stuff." I say this last part while staring at a guy in the front row and waving my arms.

"But no matter how serious you are with a girl, she will still use the lamest, most basic excuse when she wants to get rid of you. It's all the same to them. You could be married, and if the woman wanted a divorce, she'd say, I can't stay married to you anymore. I have to visit my sick grandmother.'

"That's how it was. One moment we are engaged, and then the next, I am calling her. Her roommate is like, 'she can't come to love you anymore. She's washing her hair.'" The crowd laughs. I don't pause for it. "Actually, she said, 'she is taking a final.'"

"But I said, 'We go to the same college, it's 'December 22nd and eight-thirty on a Friday night, I'm fairly sure she is not taking a final." I sit back down on the stool. "So, then I go over to her parents' house. Her dad answers the door and tells me she is not there. But behind him, she is crawling on the floor.

"I started to get suspicious after that." The crowd laughs. "I wondered if maybe she was trying to avoid me.

"Finally, she calls me." I am making this part up. "She says she can't marry me and that she's going to school in Virginia.

"I said, 'We have been through a lot. You need some space and time alone.'

"She said..." I try to muster an indignant expression, but I feel my face look hurt. They must see this is not a made-up story. "She said, 'No, it's you.'" The crowd laughs, and the laughter develops into applause.

"So I'm going to tell you right now- never underestimate what people will do to avoid their problems." That statement sits too long, so I go for something absurd. "Look at superheroes. People think they fight for truth, justice, and the American way, but they are just getting their kicks. Otherwise, why do all the superheroes have two identities? It's not to protect themselves. No. The bumbling loser is their true selves, and they dress up to get away from their crappy lives.

"Clark Kent could save people wearing a nice tie and a pair of slacks. But his life sucks. Ole Clark is so mild-mannered that Lois Lane is always scooping him and, quite frankly, blue balling him. But then he puts on tights, and suddenly he is blue-walling her and out saving her ass. If he was only out to help people, why does he take the time to change outfits before saving someone?

"It's for the attention. I suppose, though, as Clark Kent, people would sue him and make him pay for the bus he threw at a bad guy. But as his alter ego, he's free to do as he wants. No one is showing up at the fortress of solitude with a court summons.

"Spiderman is the same way. In high school, he was picked on. He's broke. He's got an ass for a boss, and his grandma is always ragging on him, as Peter Parker. But as Spiderman, he's hanging from the ceiling and throwing out one-liners. As Peter Parker, Mr. Jameson has him groveling, but Spiderman doesn't take that crap. He'll web-sling your ass and leave you hanging from a flagpole on a high building.

"It has to be great to just make yourself into someone else. Superheroes even talk in the third person because they start believing their own stuff. 'Spiderman is not so bad,' Peter Parker is always saying. 'He's just got a bad rap.' And remember the Batman TV show? Batman was always saying, 'Bruce Wayne is a friend of mine. I can get that message to him.'

"God, Batman is the worst. He doesn't even have superpowers. He just hated being Bruce Wayne, so he became Batman. Because his life sucked. Sure he has money, but he's holed up in that big house with only Alfred and his homosexual tendencies. But bam. He puts on a black suit, and suddenly he's 'The Batman!' He's out on the town, and he's wanted. Commissioner Gordon is always calling him up. Does anyone call for Bruce Wayne? No, because he is a paranoid loner. But as Batman, he even has women naming themselves after him. There's no Wayne Girl.

"My favorite, though, is the Incredible Hulk. Does David Banner turn into The Hulk when someone needs help? No. Only when he gets pissed. Good and pissed. Which is the best. Don't make me angry. You wouldn't like me when I'm angry. I'll kick your ass and smash through a wall. Only you can't blame me. It will be the Incredible Hulk. Bring it up with him. He won't give a crap. He doesn't even like me, and I am him.

"Everyone has ulterior motives. Maybe that's my point." Somehow I've saved my set. The audience is laughing again. "Clark Kent was just trying to get out of work and avoid Lois Lane's work tantrums. Which everyone has a jerk at their workplace they try to avoid. Just remember, if your co-worker shows up for work tomorrow in blue tights and won't explain why you're probably the jerk.

"Well, my time is up." I have no idea if it is or it isn't. There is nobody tonight to give me the signal with a flashlight. "But if you are looking to have kids and your standards aren't too high, I'll be at the bar after my set." I get nice applause. Then because there is no emcee tonight, just me and the comic that put this night together for Hotshots, I introduce the headliner. "I've known the next comic for a long time. John and I did a lot of open mikes together. He took me under his wing and taught me how to do standup. And on the nights we weren't trying to make it big, we were here at Hotshots trying to make it with women out of our league." The crowd cheers. "Everyone, please welcome John Johnson."

John runs up on stage and shakes my hand, then gives me a hug. "I love this guy," he says, patting my chest. Later, we will stand around and trade old stories for a while, and then we will say we should get together, but we won't. Telling old stories is not a friendship to me, and we are done making stories together. "Good to see you, Mikey," John whispers before I duck off the stage.

My fresh cigarette tastes like mucus. I'm definitely sick. When I go to the bar to get a Coke, the bartender tells me Dave is here and points to where he is sitting. I motion him to meet me at the end of the bar, so we can talk while John performs.

Dave pours me a beer from his pitcher. Hopefully, he wants to talk about the women in the crowd because I want to forget my set. I cannot remember how many things I am trying not to remember these days.

"My performance sucked ass." I keep my voice down because we should be listening to John up on stage.

"What? You were great," Dave tells me.

"It sucked dead rabbit."

"You were funny."

I'm drinking fast. Except for when peer pressure got the best of me, I was not much of a drinker. But I have to stop my serious thoughts. This wants to strike me as funny- that I have just done a stand-up routine, and I need to lighten up, but I do not let it. "I never told a joke as a kid. But in college, being funny came easy to me.

"I wished I remembered my college days," Dave says, "I was stoned for five years."

Dave doesn't understand. He is only half-comprehending as he slides a cigarette out from his pack. Memories that keep me going seem lame spoken out loud. "Making my friends laugh was like a high to me."

"So you were the clown, the cut-up."

"No, we were all funny. We all made each other laugh. The only difference was that my friends got real jobs and married."

Dave looks around the bar, checking out the women in the audience. "It sounds like it was a lot of fun." The crowd gives John the biggest roar of laughter of the night.

"That's why stand-up felt so right. I wanted to be around laughter all the time. Especially when I caused it.

"You were a pretty popular guy, huh?" He has known me long enough to know popular describes what he was in college, not me. Popular is having girls call your dorm room looking for you and rushing up to you at parties and clutching your arm.

The head of the next beer Dave pours for me swirls back into an amber solid. I need to tell him that having those friends wasn't enough. And how it was more than I have now. But I need to keep that to myself. The thing to explain right now is how I can't do comedy anymore. "Humor allowed me to fit in. It was something I was good at. I was able to get a lot of work at the clubs around here. Even after college, I never had to take temp jobs. And I've worked the last hundred and seventy-nine days out of a hundred and eighty-seven. But since I got these gigs back in Minnesota..." I need to tell him that only happy people are the ones that can tell jokes. "Things have gone to shit for me."

"Yeah, Minnesota will do that for you." Dave looks at me. He watches me take a drink. Then he tops off my glass and pours out the last of the pitcher into his glass.

John is onstage talking about people from Minnesota going to Wisconsin to buy beer on Sundays. "Aren't you happy, Mikey?" Dave's question surprises me. He's never gone from being an awkward freshman to feeling loved, only to have something happen that ruins all the good times you've ever had. He doesn't even know about going from a gig on Sunday and not talking to anyone until you come on stage for a gig on Wednesday night. It must seem to Dave that everyone is happy. "Because you will be famous someday, while I'll still be teaching."

"That guy up there." I point to John. "He's happy. He's about to go into his routine about being married. His wife is in the audience. They've had me out to their house in Eagan. He has what it takes to be a famous comedian. A nice normal, mainstream life that his audience can relate to." Suddenly, I feel the vibration of noise going into my ear, but I cannot hear the laughter of the audience or the bartenders making their noises- opening the cooler doors, shoving glasses into ice, calling out the total for drinks ordered. I can't hear myself say, "Because nothing seems funny to me anymore."

Panic makes me stand up. Dave doesn't notice my distress. He must assume I'm getting the next pitcher. The sounds around me untwist, and everything sounds louder but normal.

Dave is talking. "- a slump. You know someday you'll say that was the period of time just before this really great thing happened."

The bartender did notice me. With a nod, he gets us another of the same, and this allows me to sit down. "Good times don't just follow bad times."

"Why don't you come to church with me? It helps me stay centered. To see the important things in life."

At first, I think he is doing a setup for a joke. Because during impromptu roundtables, Dave could always quote chapter and verse from the Bible and then make a joke about it. But he also has a routine on finding God, and it's just like Dave not to hold anything back.

"Listen, last time I talked to God, some words were exchanged. He said some things. I said some things. And I meant mine."

"Yeah, been there, too. But I'm not going to press."

He gives me a Billy Graham smile that makes me angry. "You know, for a guy that goes to church on Sunday, you sure do a lot of sinning."

"Changing the subject, huh?" he says, but I didn't change the subject. Did I? He goes on, anyway. He can't tell that I didn't want a response. "Finding God has given me a lot, and I finally learned how to be happy. But I don't believe in all that stuff in the Bible. The men who wrote it had a lot of hang-ups. God gave us nerve endings in our naughty parts for us to enjoy them." He laughs. "And I am not one to waste a gift."

"The gift that keeps on giving, eh?"

"Mikey, going to church got me through a rough time. A time when my wife divorced me, and my two daughters disowned me. That's why I mentioned it. You should come with me."

"You're cracked. Do you know that, Dave?"

"Yeah. But it works for me, and it can work for you."

We listen to John tell a joke about his wife but makes himself the butt of it. Then he goes on to talk about his kids, his neighbors, and his neighbor's kids. His routine is almost over, and I will go ask the crowd, "Isn't he great?" Then I will close the show.

"I had all that your friend is talking about," Dave says. "It should have been enough for me. I make jokes about my wife and run her down, but it was me. She's the one that left, but I had already told myself my marriage was terrible and that I could do better."

"At least you had what he has. Choosing to throw it away is different from never having it at all. It's the opposite. Plus, now you still have your kids." He's talking like he has never talked about his divorce before. "And all your girlfriends."

"Someday, I'm going to use it all in a routine. Isn't that why we do standup? As a cathartic exercise?"

"No, we do it to get laid. Isn't that what you always tell me? Anyway, John is waiting for me to go up and close the show with him. Are you going to stay? We just have to get our checks from the manager after the show."

"It's either I stay or go home and do lesson plans for summer school on Monday."

I leverage myself on the arms of the stool and get off it. "Be back in a moment." I'm determined to come back and play my role of a comedian.

8

My memory

Mikey sat in the University of Minnesota Veterinary Service waiting room with people talking into pet carriers or holding onto dogs on leashes. He was as good as he was going to get with a new sweater and a fresh haircut. "God," he prayed silently. "Please let this go good and have this work. Amen."

When one of the students called the name Ted E. Bear for the next examination, Mikey stood up and walked into the examination room without an animal in tow.

He caught a glimpse of Karen before he jumped up on the table and put his hands and feet up in the air like a content puppy. She leaned in as she often did to examine a kitten, and his hands and legs fell to the surface. She was almost frumpy in a sweatshirt with a puppy on it and her lab coat. But she was also beautiful. And the blush on her freckled cheeks told him she felt the same way he did.

Mikey laid on his side and propped his head up with his hand. "So what can you do for me, Doctor?"

Karen laughed. She turned a darker red as she said, "It says here this is supposed to be neutering. But I think maybe I should hold off."

Karen looked away as she told her joke. "I don't normally ask my patients this, I don't normally ask my patients any questions, but is there something I can do for you today?"

Mike felt his heart pound. He hadn't planned on being embarrassed. "There is. To stay healthy, I need to run with my pack, but it's been a little scattered lately. There is one in my pack particularly that is becoming a loner."

The examination table was high enough, and Karen was short enough that they were eye to eye. She was close enough to him that he felt like he did when the girl at Cost Cutters leaned into him to reach the top of his head.

"I know. I really miss you guys. But I am struggling with my Neurobiology class."

"Then prescribe yourself going out with us tonight."

"I can't do prescriptions yet."

"I'll do it then." The way she was staying close to him was driving Mikey crazy. He wanted to kiss her.

"This totally brightened up my day," she said. "I can't believe you did this."

"See the extent I'll go to see you. Say you'll come."

"If I was smarter, Mikey, I wouldn't have to study so much. I miss you guys a lot too."

"Well, you'll have to see me here. I'll keep coming back and make appointments to see you."

He had been instantly attracted to her when they met three months ago. For the first time, they were alone, and her small ears under a simple bob, her upturned nose set slightly askew between hazel eyes, and her small mouth with its tightly set teeth seemed more perfect.

Karen gazed down at her boots. "Why don't you come during lunch instead? Like at eleven-thirty if you don't have class."

"Not one I actually go to, anyway." A voice told him to lean in and kiss her. "I suppose you have to get back to work."

"Yeah." She led him out the door and gave him a long hug. They broke apart. Several of Karen's classmates stood in the waiting room watching them and whispered to each other with smiles on their faces. He wished he had kissed her, but as was becoming his habit, he looked to his audience for validation. Her friends' faces told him he had done well.

9

Dan picks up the phone when I call Alaine. "Oh, it's you," he says. "I'll get her."

"No, actually, I want to talk to you. We are different people, but I've always admired you from afar." He sets the phone down. "And I've seen you stealing glances at me too." I hear the crackle of the receiver sliding along a surface as it is picked up. "And I am not going to fight my feelings anymore. Dan, I want you."

Alaine sighs. "Cut it out, Mikey."

"Oh, it's you now. Can you put Dan back on the line? Him and me was talking."

She ices me. Her lack of response is to tell me she doesn't want the joke to go on any longer. "Well, did you kill last night?"

"Merely nicked them," I say, irritated, just because she is using trade slang. I get even more irritated when she tells me all about her friend at work who called in sick and the fight she got into with Dan over the amount of money she spent shopping. Finally, she says, "Anything new with you?"

"Well, last night, it occurred to me that Karen talked to you about what happened." I try to sound casual because it's ancient history.

"Mikey, you know what happened."

"Yeah. It just occurred to me that she talked to you about it." This is the last thing I should bring up with Alaine. With Alaine and me, there should only be good times. I don't want Alaine to think Karen still lingers in my mind. My set last night, though, won't leave me alone.

"Mikey, stop beating yourself up. If she talked to me, it was a long time ago. I do know she didn't want to hurt you."

I let her lie. "It's okay. I was just looking for a reason to call you."

She doesn't say anything for a moment. "Is it still bothering you, Mikey?"

My apartment is so quiet. "No. It was a trivia question. For a hundred points and the win, why did Karen rip out my heart?" I laugh. "Seriously, it was an excuse to bother you."

"Hmmm."

Her response means she doesn't want to take the time to press. "Okay? I'll let you go."

"If you're sure. Dan wants to go somewhere for dinner." I picture Dan in basketball shorts and a T-shirt sitting on the couch watching the Cubs on WGN.

"Say goodbye to Dan for me." I hang up. Why did I ask her that? Even Alaine will think I'm crazy now. She's the only person that cares about me, and I need to hang on to her.

There was no reason to bring any of it up. I called Karen last night after not being able to sleep. Actually, I called her parents' house first. Her dad answered the phone. He knew it was me and that I was drunk, but he was polite. He simply said, "Karen lives in Virginia now."

Then I called her number mined from the phone books in the library. I asked her how she was doing and what she was up to. She said, "Nothing." Then I asked her if she had been sleeping. "Yes," she had replied.

I regretted it as soon as she picked up, but I stayed on the line. Her voice, always scratchy as if she had a perpetual cold, shocked my whole body. It was so familiar – I listened to it so often in the warm darkness of lying in bed next to her. Her voice sent quivers of anticipation through my body, then anger. Yet every part of me waited for her next word so I could lay my head down on her voice's lap. We haven't talked in six months, and she didn't want to talk to me, but she didn't hang up.

"Mikey, you must be doing well, right?" she said when I didn't say anything for a while. "My parents told me you're going on tour. They read in the entertainment section of the Tribune that you would be out here doing some big clubs in New York and Atlanta."

"Well, in October." Doing good. How did she mean that? Did I get out of the local scene, and am I making more money? Yeah. Does that mean I am doing good? That I am all right, and everything turned out for the best? I hope that's not what you meant, Karen.

"Good. I am glad about that."

I wish she had hung up on me. We are eleven hundred miles away. Was it too much to think she might say something that proved she had loved me at one time? A stranger could ask me if I was doing good.

10

It's about an hour and a half drive to the Whistle Stop Station in Saint Cloud, where I'm working the next few nights. The Beast is sucking down gas, and the worn-out front end is shaking. I should stop calling my car that. I'm too old to have a name for inanimate objects. When Alaine named the car, we were at the age where we were adults but didn't have to act like ones. We did things like sit on the hoods of cars and sing along to the radio. Now she is past that age, but I'm not. My face is pressed flat against the plastic sheet that separates me from the present. I am still in the past, clinging to the last bit of my hope.

People talking on cell phones and driving big SUVs whiz by me. I roar by old Chevys and Fords loaded down with kids. I'd rather be any of the people around me. But I'm more jealous of the person with the kids driving to Chucky Cheese or driving to their hectic, loud, full homes.

Okay, I think in my therapist voice. You're in a little negative spiral right now. My head is groggy from taking cold medicine and falling asleep. Waking up at six, I only had time to grab my keys and leave. The car was heading west before I realized I'm wearing jean shorts and a shapeless tank top. Which is great for a man with toned arms, but I'm fucked. The hair on my shoulders looks like razor wire, and the crowd will not be happy to see a hairy nip slip. For that matter, I planned on never being in a situation where anyone saw the jungles in my armpits. Replaying the phone call with Alaine adds to the cornucopia of things making me morose.

Alaine was the first friend I made at college. We signed up on a bulletin board to share rides to and from Duluth. It was a way to meet someone more than to share a ride. I was shy, and the guys on my dorm wing seemed so different. They drank and smoked pot, and I did neither. My roommate was never there and then dropped out. That left me alone in my small dorm room a lot, so, until Alaine, college had not been any different than the rest of my life.

I expected to be in contact with a guy – somebody from Duluth or Superior that I could hang around with. I couldn't help but hope he had a cute sister. When Alaine contacted me, yes, I thought she was beautiful. She was so outgoing and light-hearted; we had so much fun talking on the trips back and forth that I fantasized about going out with her. But I never asked her. I had learned from the many times I hit it off with a pretty girl. Those girls, classmates in high school, seemed so happy to know me because I was "so nice." I had strong feelings for them, and they did for me, but I wasn't good-looking enough to date. Except for not wanting to be seen in public with me, I had everything these girls wanted. That is what it came down to.

But I just liked Alaine, too. I regarded the things we did together as purer because we were friends, and I wasn't looking for anything more than her companionship. We saw each other every day, and because of her, I had the confidence to make a bunch of friends.

Our relationship didn't change when she began dating Dan. It was still the perfect friendship. I did feel like an ex-boyfriend around him, but Alaine didn't treat me any differently. And he didn't try to steal her away from me and our friends. He had his own clique. They would start at their bar, and Alaine went out with us. We got her until we ended up at the bar where Dan and his buddies hung out. Then we would all hang out, and I was the clown who got everybody laughing.

Between trying to keep the car on the road and remembering how things aren't now, I am miserable by the time I get to Whistle Stop Station.

Once on the stage, the lights excite and calm me. Not like they used to. I have always been able to escape up on stage and in the jokes. Up here, I don't have to think about anything else. I am the life of the party, and the audience members are my friends. Since my first open mike, stand-up has been the Valium for the part of me that needed to relax and the Prozac for the part that needed cheering up.

The stage doesn't do that for me anymore. Perhaps I have built up a tolerance and need to up the dose. Still, my set is going all right. "So I am in the check-out lane," I tell the good size audience. "My arms are getting tired from holding my balanced meal of a frozen pizza and carton of cigarettes." I take a dramatic pause to give them time to laugh, which they don't do.

"Hey, Bigfoot," somebody calls out. "Even Bigfoot is doing stand-up now."

My hand goes to my chin because I haven't shaven for a long time. For a moment, I don't know what to do. I haven't braced myself for hecklers. So, I do nothing other than feel sorry for myself. Shit. Why would I leave the house like this? My arms reflexively cross, but the audience still sees the thick hair on my chest. My legs are long, fat logs rolled in pubic hair. The heckler needs to be put in his place, but I can't even think of the standard comebacks. So I jump up and growl.

"What makes you call me Bigfoot?" The crowd loves it.

But my heckler loves that he got a response from me. "Cause your so frickin' huge," he replies.

I'm pissed at the last comic for making the joke, "Your momma is so hairy, Bigfoot took her picture." I am pissed at this heckler, my life, Alaine. "Yeah, that's what your wife said last night," I say, trying to sound like Bobcat Goldthwaite. I growl and beat my chest, strutting back and forth on the stage. Then I run off, not knowing what else to do. The comic that is the emcee tonight comes up on stage and looks at me as I stand in the back of the room. I still have ten minutes to do, but drag my finger across my throat.

The emcee stretches out his closing material a little while I pace in the bathroom, and then the audience leaves. Guys come in to relieve themselves of anything over the two-drink minimum before driving home, so I wash my hands and walk out.

I sit at the bar so the manager can find me if he wants to. I light a cigarette and will people not to come up to me.

The bartender sets a drink in my line of vision. "Good show." She has large waves of thick, light-brown hair with teased bangs.

"Thanks," I mumble, instantly attracted to her deep tan and sparkling hazel eyes. Her sleeveless denim shirt is tight around her chest, and her top buttons are undone to expose the tan, freckled valley between two round breasts.

"The part at the end was great."

"Yeah, right." I was heckled and humiliated. "It was crazy."

"I like crazy," she says.

"Then you'll love me." I intended this as sarcasm, but it doesn't come out that way. It comes out as flirting.

Her hand tucks a strand of hair behind her ear. Then she takes care of a couple of customers. It gives me time to see that guys hit on her all the time. When the guys tell her something, she gives them all a wide smile.

She has a small beer belly. It's sexy as it strains against the denim, and I can't stop looking at the tight shorts she's wearing. She catches me checking her out but looks into my eyes and smiles, and my heart pounds. When she comes back. I grab a twenty out of my pocket and toss it on the bar. "Another one there, Bigfoot?" She has one for me already and doesn't take my money.

I growl like an animal. It's all I can think to do, but hate being called that. The guy next to me tugs on her arm playfully. I miss what he says, but she reaches across the bar and lightly slaps his head. I stare at her shirt tight across her chest. Her sexiness makes me as skittish as a fawn but unable to look away.

She has the looks that always make me get quiet and act weird because it is absurd for a guy like me to flirt with a girl like her. A sexy woman must be judging me as out of her league. Any time a beautiful woman talks to me, I figure they are playing a joke.

But right now, I don't care because things can't get worse. If she keeps talking to me, then I don't have to go home. And maybe she's truthful when she says she likes crazy.

"Thanks for the drink," I say when she parks herself at my corner of the bar. As the night goes on, her tan, her hair, and her tight clothes are attracting the attention of all the guys, but she ignores everything but their drink orders and our conversation.

In response to a few questions I ask, she reveals she's lived in Saint Cloud all her life, has three older brothers, and played the clarinet in high school. At first, I am interested to know these things, but the more I see and smell her, my listening intently is simply to keep her close.

"I'm Janet." She rocks back and forth on her heels. This tells me she was waiting for me to ask. Normally, I get to know the staff at the clubs, but I'm so in shock that she is talking to me, I forgot to ask her name. "Tonight, you're drinking for free, Mikey."

We joke around until closing time.

"I'm going to be here a while," she says as people file out. "Come talk to me after the show tomorrow."

11

Alaine calls at eleven AM. She leaves me a message about meeting for lunch, but I do not call her back. Instead, I spend the day on my couch, lusting after Janet. With fantasies of getting her naked, I jack off twice. But in that self-loathing period afterward, I compare her to Alaine, and she doesn't measure up. This confuses me because I can't bring myself to fantasize about Alaine.

"It's Bigfoot," someone calls out just before my closing line. The guy from last night got such a big laugh that I think it might be him. That was the other thing I thought about all day. What was it about me that made the guy call me that? As a kid, I sometimes felt there was something un-human about me and that the rest of the world knew it. But being called a monster two nights in a row freaks me out.

Okay, I've gotten weirder being on the road for six months. I've gotten used to being alone, and I'm different than when I left. Is it noticeable?

My heckler doesn't reveal himself. In the past, I would have stopped my set until I had goaded him into showing himself and then slammed him because, unlike other comics, I did not have to worry about the guy starting a fight after the show. Depending on who was heckling me, I might even engage in some banter, so he had something to brag about at work. But tonight, I will give my response to his heckle, finish my set, and be done. "You got it wrong there, brain surgeon. I'm Big Dick. His more popular cousin."

It's my biggest laugh of the night, so I add, "More popular with your wife at any rate." But I come off the stage psyched-out. I've been heckled about being fat, and I come up with ten fat jokes to the hecklers one before giving him the line about not coming down to where he works and knocking the dick out of his mouth. But being called something not human is something I can't handle right now.

The emcee is onstage, closing the show. I head toward the bar and Janet. She is every man's idea of a fun date. Well, not for a guy like me. Sexiness radiates from her. Other men see that sexy quality as a message that says *conquer me*. The message to me is *not on your best day*.

So, all day, I rechecked the events of last night to see if I got things wrong. But there was the chemistry that only happens when both people are attracted. It's the anticipation of what comes next and leads to the next high of physical connection. Will that happen? No. For the first time, though, I am not disappointed to be coming off the stage and lumbering to the bar.

Then someone yells out, "Hey, Bigfoot." In an instant, I turn my direction, walk to the door, and out into the night. Escape, I think. Everyone here sees me as a monster. I fumble to get my car started, light a cigarette, and pull out of the parking lot.

I can't go back in now. It's trivial, a joke. But as soon as that jerk yelled out "Bigfoot," I couldn't spend the night with those words wafting around in my head. Janet would have spent the whole night calling me Bigfoot or even big guy. I can never just be a person like everyone else. Thin, medium-tall Mike with good hair doesn't exist.

The cigarette tastes like rotting seeds, but smoke must fill me so I can drive home.

On I94, each mile clicking off on the odometer tells me to go back, but with each mile, it is more impossible to do. I rub my face with my fingertips over and over. How did I lose control of the stage? And how did I get such a heavy beard so fast?

Somatic mutations. The term from some health or psychology class pops into my head. It changes someone's genes throughout their life, and that changes them. It makes me think of my dad. He started out with me and mom, and now he is twice divorced and lives alone in a trailer out in the woods. Maybe I'm following my genes.

The lights of businesses and billboards of 494 flash next to me. The Northwest Hanger reminds me of my tour in October. As a headliner in big East Coast venues, I get to fly to my shows. Envisioning this, I also saw Karen coming to one of my big shows and then my driver taking us some place to talk. It will not happen. A successful comic can't be this stupid.

* * *

My big, empty apartment. Everything about me is big and empty. The possibility of going out with Janet is gone. What she saw was me finishing my set and simply ignoring her. What excuse could I have? Ah, sorry, I had to leave because a heckler questioned my genotype, and it got me worrying about it.

What would have happened if I had groomed properly? What if we had hit it off a second night? In other words, what if Janet got to know me? Eventually, she would reject me. But a relationship with her would let me forget about my love for Alaine, and then Alaine and I could still be friends. If Janet somehow didn't reject me, I wouldn't have to fall in love too much. We could be together until Alaine and Dan break up, and then I'd have another chance to be with Alaine.

The TV is on, but the sound is down. Black and white images of an old movie stare back. In time, I forget that people have voices. These people live in a silent world, but they don't know anything else.

I need out of this apartment. Even if it's just to stand out in the hall. I do not move until it is time to light another cigarette.

With indecision and heavy limbs, I get up and put my shoes on. Exhaustion wants to drag me back to the couch, but I pilfer through my suitcase still in the living room and pull out a plain dark-blue sweatshirt and jeans. After managing to put them on with a cigarette in my mouth, I notice the blinking light of my answering machine.

It's Alaine. "Mikey. You are still probably in Saint Cloud but call me when you get home. Even if it's late. You're home, and we haven't spent any time together. It also seems like you're mad at me. Maybe I'm crazy, but—" She takes a deep breath and exhales. "That is simply not acceptable. So call me. Okay? Love ya."

At twelve-thirty, my neighborhood is silent. The apartment building stands cold in the darkness and fades away as I walk. I keep looking back at it because it is part of my identity. The square old apartment building says I have no other place to be.

Houses soon surround me with their heavy brows over double-paned eyes. They watch me, the outsider, ready to summon help if I try anything.

Everything is still and quiet. "Fuck," I cry out, mostly mouthing the word. I got out of my apartment to put distance between me and my thoughts. But emotions and thoughts bombard me all at once. Another big guy is sitting at the bar talking to Janet. If he goes home with her, it's because she expected to spend time with me after my set. The same will happen with my career. Paying my dues and performing for free has led to success, but something will happen just as I'm about to take it to the next level. Then some other burly comic will replace me.

My career will parallel my relationships. They were great until I counted on them. Then I fumbled and faltered, and they crumbled as

I scrambled to hold on to all the pieces. I will not do that with my act. Or with anything. Everything can just fall away.

But why did those hecklers call me a monster? All my lonely times growing up, I cursed myself for being different. For being ugly. Ugly to everyone eventually.

Except for Alaine. I stand on the sidewalk to think about how good she is. Good enough to see beyond my ugliness.

She hasn't given up on me. That phone call proves she loves me. She will be my last chance. Perhaps coming home and having everything be at a dead-end, including the hope of going out with someone new, had to happen to force me to act. I have nothing to lose and any amount of love to gain at this point.

I will tell Alaine that I love her. She doesn't really want to marry Dan. And if I can end up with her, then all I have gone through will be for something.

12

"I don't like it," Alaine says, sitting across the booth. She tightens the sweater around her because the air-conditioning is making her cold. Her light fragrance takes me back to our Sunday afternoon commutes to the twin cities just after Alaine went out to lunch with her parents. "It makes you so scruffy, especially with that long hair."

This opinion puts me at a disadvantage to tell her of my love. In our phone conversations in the last month, I had to stop myself from admitting my love for her. But now, I keep saying things that get me farther away from the right time to tell her.

I invited her to lunch because I couldn't wait until dinner. That gave time for my declaration of love to sink in before she saw Dan. But I didn't shave or even check a mirror to make myself presentable.

"Yeah, but I met a chick who digs my beard." Way to flirt with her, Mikey. Bring up another woman. It was a silly attempt to sound like I had options. I can never even flirt with Janet again, but my lie of being normal may as well be based on a small chip of reality.

But it doesn't make me sound any less desperate. It just drives a wedge between me and what I want. But today has to be the day. Despite the beard and mentioning another woman. Despite the fact she has twenty-three minutes left of her lunch break to realize she loves me.

Rash words come out of my mouth. It seems like someone else's hands lifting the food up and someone else's mouth chewing.

"Ohh." Alaine is poking her plastic fork into her salad. She moves an egg slice off to the side and cuts her tomato wedge in half. "A chick, huh? So, tell me, what's she like?"

"Well, she's got big tits." I lean back like that is my definition of a good woman. Alaine furrows her brow as she chews. She is tormenting me, and I want her stirred up and on edge, too.

Janet's chest is also the first thing that comes to my mind. For an instant, I see myself making love to Janet. It surprises me. Masturbating aside, my attraction for a woman came from a stirring in my heart. I relished the emotions a woman evoked in me and then found her sexiness. It was always waiting to be seen by an eye that did not compare her to an ideal. But right now, I have a vision of this woman who is really just a stranger, and I can describe her breasts like I own them.

"That's nice," Alaine says. "Firm and round?"

"Oh, you've met her?" I dip a French fry into a small paper cup holding ketchup. Alaine takes a few healthy bites of her salad. I can't look at Alaine for fear I will stare at the swells of her own chest wrapped tightly in her sweater.

She looks at me. Groans.

"What?"

"At least tell me her name."

I stuff fries into my mouth and chew. For a moment, I can't remember the woman's name. Without wanting to, my shoulders shrug. Alaine stares at me. "Cut it out. You know I don't like humor like that. It's degrading–"

"Janet," I finally say. "I really don't know her that well."

"Really."

"She tends bar at Whistle Stop Station, and she thinks I'm crazy." Alaine slides the fork along her teeth as she takes a bite of lettuce. At this moment, I only want her to experience discomfort. She knows what I want to tell her and is making me work for her love.

She looks directly into my eyes, startling me. "Mikey, I know you're going through a rough time right now. And you won't talk about it. So, I hope you get something going with Janet. You deserve it."

I look away, across the restaurant.

She says, "It's just that I'm worried about you. You know I love ya, ya big lug."

"Of course." I force myself to make eye contact. She puts her hand on mine. "I'm lost without that."

"And you love me, don't you, buddy?" She smiles and caresses my hand.

Here is my last chance. She is not treating me well right now, but I know the real her. She deserves to be told I love her and that she has saved me from going crazy from loneliness a thousand times. It has to happen before we leave the restaurant, or she will never know.

Alaine needs my declaration to trigger something in her and make her realize she loves me in a dangerous way. Perhaps it is impossible. She is too good to hurt Dan and admit this truth. The way she calls me buddy tells me she wants to love me like a pet. "I will always be by your side. Wagging my tail and fetching sticks for you."

She has me walk her back to her office. People in business suits are scattered around Saint Paul's downtown. Decked out in success and happiness, Men and women eat their lunch by the river or in front of the courthouse. Some kick off their shiny shoes, and other smoke while leaning back. Alaine is one of these chosen people. "Mikey, you still haven't told me what is going on with you," she says. "I hope you can share things with Janet, and you'll let her be there for you."

It hurts me. How can she be next to me, know how I love her, yet try to pawn me off on some other woman?

"I am glad you found someone. Even better that she lives here. I was so afraid you would fall in love with some girl on the road and move away. Actually, when you didn't come home at all, I assumed you had found a girlfriend."

"No," We walk to get her back on time. "Those few times I had a string of days off, I meandered toward my next gig, driving and staying in cheap motels without talking to anyone but the people at the front desk and a voice through a drive-thru speaker."

"It sounds lonely."

"It was."

"You could have called me more, Mikey."

"I was being tough not doing that." The truth is it was good to subject myself to the loneliness. Sometimes, I took off and headed in a random direction, but it wasn't an adventure. It was exhausting. I would never end up even getting out of the car; I would get lost, and getting lost feels the same no matter where you are.

"Mikey, if you don't enjoy being on the road, then don't do it. Stay here and settle down with Janet or whoever you fall in love with."

But it would be better to move away. I could go on loving Alaine, and we would never have to admit what is going on between us. I'd rather be tormented than rejected. Love is just a game God makes to hurt people, anyway.

"My kids are going to need their Uncle Mikey."

I see her out of the corner of my eye. Alaine is looking at me with concern on her face. She slips her arm around mine as she has many times before, but I pry my arm off to get away from this taunt.

It's hard for us to stay together, weaving through people at the corner. For some reason, she is mistreating me, but I am compelled to make sure she gets to her building. She is my best friend and the best person I've ever known. We come to her office building.

"Mike, I didn't mean to say that. I was trying to make you feel better. You won't tell me what's the matter, but I've never seen you so on edge."

It's because it's a terrible thing to hope for love. "Yeah, I'm fine. Sorry." I manage to sound like a normal human being. Drips of sweat slide down my armpits. My faces itches.

"Are you okay?" She looks into my eyes again. I avoid the confrontation.

"I'm ggggggreat!" I say like Tony the Tiger and step into a crowd of business suits walking back to their offices. With long strides, I overtake little, happy people.

Two blocks from Alaine, I slow down. My mind wants to fly through the crowd and exhaust itself, but my body is already exhausted and feverous again. With no place to go, I must keep walking.

My emotions have been wrung out again. I spread them over Karen's pain like a jacket over a puddle. She muddied and stomped them into the muck and then looked away when I tried to gather them back into me. Alaine is doing the same thing. I must strip her away, scrape her out of me.

I have left the downtown people behind and keep walking without knowing what direction I am headed. This leaves me with no one, but I have always been separate. Even when I wiggled into groups by being funny, I was still different. From now on, I will want separateness.

Distance is what I need, and to be lost. I walk through the tall buildings and the businesses until the street transitions to an older, poorer neighborhood. The houses overflow with belongings so that their porches are full of their excess couches and bags of clothes and toys for their children, who would rather have a porch floor to play on. I duck the low-hanging branches from the well-established maple trees that anchor this neighborhood down. They do not camouflage me, though. The green and shadows of urban nature are to protect small animals. Not an elk rutting through town.

The houses get newer and nicer and more homogenous. They are also more familiar and remind me a park is nearby. The vision of an open space spurs me on to go lie down on the grass like a kid and watch the clouds until my exhaustion passes.

Above me is an ordinary blue sky. I stop and search for a single cloud that will allow me to place my soul on it and float it away. There is only emptiness above.

The lawns become larger and the trees younger, and that gives me a sign I am near the park. Karen and I drove through this neighborhood after a few weeks of dating and thought it the perfect place to raise a family.

And then I come upon the corner of a block with a playground. A baseball diamond is in the back corner. Fenced-in yards are beyond that. There are two small shelters with picnic tables near the playground equipment. I survey it all from the knoll in the middle of the park. It is quiet, and I realize that until now, the noise of the downtown remained in my head.

The park is empty, but I am too embarrassed to lie down on the hill. All I can do is sit and watch for someone to come into the park because I will get up and walk off.

The sky has expanded, but there still aren't any clouds to make into something with your mind.

I replay the night with Janet at the bar. My words as I avoided my confession to Alaine repeat in my head. Karen hides as her dad answers the door and tells me she is not home. These will go on haunting me. At least there will not be anymore. Today was my last chance for something good.

The sunlight is too bright through my closed eyelids. These thoughts cannot be stopped from penetrating either. On the road, I was busy driving, eating, doing my laundry, and hanging out with other unlikeable comics. I kept so busy, but my stupidity has been waiting at home.

God, I was an idiot to think Alaine would fall in love with me. Didn't I learn from Karen that things don't ever work out? I should have stayed on the road where Karen did not exist for more than a few passing moments. Our breakup should not be hitting me after six months.

A mother has brought her toddler into the park. She has unloaded him from the stroller and is pushing him in a baby swing. After a few pushes, she steps to the side and bends down. She is talking to him. The baby's arms fling out with joy.

A long-distance relationship while I was on the road would not have been easy. Karen must have worked out the details of our future and decided we would not have lasted the two years while she completed graduate school. There was sorrow and loss between us. These thoughts lurked in my mind, pestering and yet waiting for this moment. They do not reveal themselves to be reasons, excuses, or blame. And yet they lead me to the same truth: I got too serious too fast. I pushed for marriage and showed too much of my feelings.

This makes me stand up. I must stand up. If that mother and child see me sitting here, they will get afraid. On the way to get out of the park, I pass the island of small trees and shrubs behind the sign that tells the name of the park and the park rules. The mother does not notice me, so I walk into the middle of this island. I stand on wood mulch and feel the green coolness around me. Sitting down, I am among small green weeds, a couple of plastic pop bottles, and a French fry box from McDonald's,

Here is a refuge.

I only showed Karen the full force of my love for her because she needed to feel special. Her love gave me strength, and I wanted to return that gift. Well, not her love, but my mistaken belief she loved me. Through the low branches, I check on mom and baby. She is still pushing him on the swing. Perhaps the dad will join them. Each time I pushed my sisters on the swings, I thought I was creating a happy childhood for them and for myself.

Perhaps this woman is a single mom devoted to her child. The dad is not coming. My mom never took me to the park. She always said my dad never let her out of the house and that she was too busy after he left.

Every time she said this, I was relieved I had never burdened her by asking her to go places. But I always wondered how she had time for Chet and not me.

Two girls have also arrived. The older one, nine or ten, is going down the slide while the younger one, five or six, tends to the doll she has brought in a baby stroller. The ten-year-old goes down the slide several times. A cute scene until the ten-year-old goes over to the younger one and takes the doll. The little one screams, "No." She screams again, a high pitch screech to show she means business.

My hands reach out with a desire to comfort the child, but I would only frighten her. She stops screaming anyway when the older one storms to the slide. I see there was no reason to worry when the older sister goes over to the merry-go-round, and the little one follows her. The little one sits in the middle, and her sister pushes as fast as she can before jumping on. The fight was forgotten in a moment.

Exhausted, I crawl back to the middle of my island and lay down. The small pea scrubs now seem to tower over me. They envelop me, and in enough time, I will become entrenched in the cool, musty wood chips. I am an ancient creature whose only function is to lay here.

The voices of a group of kids crossing the street and walking by my new home stir me to sit up. These children would be terrified of an inert, ugly me. I crawl to the side without kids and spring out of my lair. My actions are strange, but I am not ashamed of them. It was better to be a growth on the ground than human.

Walking directly out of the park, the sun is too bright.

Going along the blocks back toward the downtown, I mentally bash my brains for hiding in the landscaping of a children's park and for thinking I shouldn't be ashamed. When I convince myself to forget about that, my other sins take their turns. The women- Karen, Alaine, and Janet- form in my brain and embarrass me. That is what I was hiding from.

The Super America gas station tells me I am near the downtown again. During the first few months of school, I drove around to fill up the evenings when my dorm mates were hanging out before going to a house party. I was driving around like a superhero looking for a girl in trouble so I could save her, and she would fall in love with me. It sounds crazy, but it's not like I had an actual plan.

Nestled in the land of tall buildings and cement surfaces of downtown St. Paul, this convenience store was like the one on Main Street Duluth. I went in to find comfort in a familiar place, but it was busy and small.

These memories are my own personal evidence that I am an idiot.

Now I head toward Super America for the anonymity of a convenience store, and it's the one place I can get something to eat without having to talk to anyone. My flu symptoms are getting worse by the moment, but the ever-present message in my head tells me food will make me feel better. The coolness of the air-conditioned aisles of consumables hits me. I sniff at the sub sandwiches in their crinkly cellophane and at the candy bars in their comforting brown and yellow wrappers, but they make me nauseous. A loaf of bread is the only thing that does not bring bile to my mouth.

As I walk, I cram six tasteless slices into my mouth and throw the rest away. It feels good to deny myself anything else. The soft bread mushes together in my mouth.

My joints feel worked dry of any lubrication. But I walk to the middle of the Navy Island Bridge over the Mississippi. Cars hum behind me. The emotions I tried to leave with Alaine and then in the park hunt me, but I am fair prey. Not a warm, caring person. After all, I pretended to have a girlfriend to lure my best friend from getting married.

I shake my head and try to erase all my problems and all my sins like an Etch-A-Sketch.

The water is golden and bright from the evening sun. Cars rumble behind me. The cool wind lashes at my bare legs now. Everything is sharp on my senses and fogs my mind. It makes me dizzy to the point of falling to my knees, but this bombardment drives my thoughts away. For too long, I tried to take everything in and catalog it in my mind for future use in a joke. And to make sense of the world. I cram the roughness of the rusty railing against my palms and the big rocks on the shore, and the exhaust fumes into my consciousness. My will snaps. It is the sound of my mom breaking a fist full of spaghetti into boiling water. This is a relief.

The bridge vibrates, and the cars barrel by, and those images take my whole mind. I concentrate on the sounds around me and jerk my head to see where each sound comes from, like a hunting cat. An animal's brain must be taken up in the moment and surviving. There is no worrying about the past or the future. Growing up, our cats panicked easily. We fretted to see their fear, but they found release in running to a hiding place.

A diesel truck goes by. A jet is low on its approach to the airport. My heartbeat pounds at my temples.

This becomes everything—the commotion around me and the functions of my body.

$$* * *$$

I have a show at eight. Even with my mind freed, something within me remembers. It sends me running. Scampering? Yes. I am too frantic to slow enough to check my watch. My new perception provides. By continuing to scan, I see a digital bank clock. 67 degrees. 6:58.

My mind is still foggy, and I cannot quite get my bearings. Knowing the time doesn't help me if I can't remember my destination. Panting and out of breath, I can only go in the direction my car might be.

Instincts take me to my car. But next will be the test. Wandering the street is no man's land. Now I have to go back to my life and remain becoming what I am becoming.

13

I am standing before the crowd. They watch me, quiet from the moment the featured comedian said, "Well, there he finally is, so I'll get off the stage and let him have the rest of his time. Please welcome, Mikey Haskell." My hair is a mess, and my clothes are sweaty. The hours of my wandering show (I can tell on the other comedian's face), but the stunned crowd gives me some applause.

"The special tonight is pork chops and applesauce," I say while approaching the microphone so that applesauce is the only word that gets amplified.

"Bigfoot," someone yells like the other night. "We've spotted Bigfoot." A group in the crowd laugh.

My reaction is not hurt or anger. A few hours ago, I was a motionless creature lying among woodchips. How am I standing here now? The crowd and the stage lights cause me to shield my eyes. My mind is emptied of every word of my act. The crowd watches me, and I watch them back, refusing to see them as any more than images through my fingers.

Until someone puts their foot on the stage. It's my goddamn stage. If these people want Big Foot, I can give it to them. I kick over the stool. It bounces and hits a guy's leg. He jumps up, and I growl at him for doing so.

"I want a piece of ass," I yell out in a voice between Ralph Kramden and Chewbacca from "Star Wars." The crowd gets quiet. "It's fuckin' lonely up in the mountains. Oh sure, I get some ass once the bears hibernate, but that ain't a challenge." I pound around on the stage, growling, pacing. The crowd laughs. Then I stop and give a guy in the third row a thousand-yard stare. This guy- medium height with curly hair, khaki shorts, and a T-shirt- was only in my line of sight.

Despite the fact, I am not saying or doing anything, the crowd cheers and churns their arms in the air like people at a sporting event. It is their symbolic violence, bringing their arms up and striking the air in front of them. They want to attack and have the power over prey but do not dare.

Well, fuck them. "Fuck you all," I say. I take a moment, an extra moment I never dared before, and soak up the crowd before me, the ceiling, and the exit signs in the back of the room. The cocktail waitresses slice through the seated crowd like farmers walking down rows of their cornfield – knee-high by the fourth of July.

My mind searches for some more crazy shit to do on the empty stage. I get down on all fours and sniff the brick wall. "Me have relatives visit here recently."

A waitress brings a table their drinks and appetizers. Her movement causes me to jump off the stage. I sniff the air and then run to the table, grabbing onion rings off her tray. "I eat now," I yell, my unamplified voice dissipating into the crowd and cram a handful of onion rings into my mouth. The crowd roars. I chew, letting breading and slippery onion spew out. I wipe my mouth with my bare arm and growl.

I grab a bottle of beer in front of a guy and lift it above me to let the liquid splash down my throat. If they want a monster, they are going to get one. I toss the bottle back onto the table. It rolls off, not breaking but bouncing end over end on the carpeted floor.

My feet come down with thuds as I jump back up on stage. To

my right, on the left of the stage, a blonde sits in front—the beautiful woman with her fat, well-dressed husband. I couldn't find the front-row woman at first. But she is only guaranteed to be there on Saturdays. I go to my knees in front of her and point to her chest. "Me want," I tell the crowd. I grab her arm and rub my hairy face up and down her arm, and growl.

She hits me on top of the head with her small hand, trying to be funny, but in a small panic. I hold on tighter. The crowd screams with laughter. It makes me growl at her. Her overweight, well-dressed companion has stood up. I am hardly aware of what I am doing, but it feels good to be doing it.

A flashlight from the back of the room signals me to stop as the guy steps toward me. Without another word to the audience, I run up the narrow aisle and bang through the swing door that leads to the kitchen. I've misjudged the small step up to it and slam to the floor. The pain sears through my body, and I am unable to do anything but turn over and pant.

A pressure on my chest opens my eyes. Janet has her boot on my chest, and I'm looking up at the crotch of her tight jeans. She smiles, looking down at me. "Let's get out of here."

The other comic is at the mike, closing the show. Janet leads me out the backdoor and to her car. She unlocks the passenger door of an old red Firebird for me and gets in her side. The engine cranks over, and the car shakes to life. She revs the engine a few times like a guy. Then she accelerates through the parking lot and onto the street without looking. After she shifts into third, she takes her hand off the shifter and plants it on the crotch of my shorts. In her grasp, I get a hard-on.

She rubs my pants. I unbutton her jeans. Nervousness and doubt exist at my fingertips, but I am not connected to them. Her zipper gives way, and I touch her pubic hair through the silk of her panties. I slip my finger into her underwear and reach down by her. We turn a corner with the tires squealing. She takes her hand away from me to shift, so I take my hand away.

We pull into a driveway. It must be hers.

Janet leads me up the wooden stairs that wind up the side of the house to her apartment. Doubt has been a bullet shot into me. Today has formed the scar tissue around it. With fear contained in this closed wound, I feel only coldness and lust. It's invigorating. We press into each other as she unlocks her door. No words come to me. I have nothing to say, but she says, "Don't talk." She kicks off her shoes and pulls her sweatshirt off. The door is still open. I pull off her jeans and underwear; then go to my knees to help her step out of them.

She drags me down into the square of moonlight on the floor. She is naked except for a bra. "You like me, don't ya, big man?" Her question is muffled in my ear. Everything around me takes the same amount of attention. Her eyes looking at me, the triangle of pubic hair, and her white mounds embraced by her peach color bra excite me. But so does her darkened apartment and the smell of a musty carpet.

She asks me another question that I do not hear. I respond, "You're great."

She undoes my jeans, and we get them off with my underwear. We get my shirt off, and she rolls on top of me. Straddles me. She reaches up to her back and undoes her bra. As she leans forward and pulls it off her rounded shoulders, her full breasts are over me. She lifts herself up, reaches between her legs, and puts me in her.

I can tell she is trying to find where it feels best for her. She makes only the slightest movements, but it makes me close to coming. Biblical scriptures and old sermons run in a narrow ribbon in front of my mind's eye. Just as they sometimes did in a judging way while making love to Karen. Instead of causing guilt, they excite me as much as her crotch rubbing on mine in the dim light.

She falls forward, and I realize she is drunk. She laughs at her slip up, but I feel the laughter toward me. I lift her back up by the shoulders. With her laughing, the closeness to coming drops out of me like somebody released the pressure in my brain and penis simultaneously. But not out of humiliation. Her laughter means nothing, and I already got what I wanted out of this. I roll over and go on top. She likes that. In the new position, I am not vulnerable. That gives me strength, and she reaps the benefits of that as I thrust into her.

A minute later, remembering random snippets of what happened on stage makes me stop. Janet reacts by running her fingers through my chest hair, and I stop caring what I did or didn't do. It got me here.

14

The phone wakes me from the floor of my dining room. I remember pulling sheets out of the hall closet and spreading them out, but not leaving Janet's or driving home. The crawl to the end table hurts my knees.

"Mikey, are you there?" Alaine's voice asks me.

"What time is it?"

"You're still asleep? It's three in the afternoon."

"Late night." I squint, allowing only a crack of light into my eyes.

"I was just calling you to see what was bothering you yesterday."

"Yeah." I struggle to stand up. My body is not ready to move. It is in a state of flux or maybe not used to running and having sex on the same day. In one day? In the same year. I hobble to the bathroom. Luckily the phone from the last tenant has a long cord. "It's not bothering me anymore," I say, peeing. The phone flies out of my hand and slides back to the living room. My image in the mirror distracts me. The fuzz of my beard and my long, flyaway hair buries my face except for my nose and eyes. Moving closer, I see each hair as it dives into the porous skin of my cheeks. Fur has taken over my face.

Of course, they called me Bigfoot. I have unlocked a secret and transformed myself into an animal. From my father, I must have a genetic disposition that puts me closer to being an animal than most people. It would account for my hairiness and my large size. Lying in the park was the incantation, and by focusing on being animalistic, I stripped away everything from myself that wasn't animal, my weaknesses. It gave me strength and power instead. Janet sensed this and liked it.

As always, my next stop after the bathroom is the kitchen. Yet the only thing I can bring myself to eat is generic corn flakes my mom threw in with those Goddamn tomato soups. The box refuses to open and forces me to rip it before scooping out handfuls and cupping them to my mouth. I go to the patio door to keep tapping into nature's freedom. The phone is making a loud beeping sound, so I hang it up. Still eating from the mound of cornflakes shelved in my hand against my stomach, I wander back to my bathroom mirror.

In it, a Bigfoot-like creature wearing a dirty tank top glares at me. His face is fuzzy with a curly beard, and he has matted hair. He smiles in satisfaction.

The phone rings again. It's probably Alaine calling to find out why I stopped talking to her. I rub the cereal crumbs off my hands with my shirt and pick up the phone.

"Hi there," Janet says. "Just me giving you a call before work. Is that okay?"

"Fine."

"What'cha doin' today?"

"Trying to get something cornered and killed."

"What? Oh." She laughs a little. "I forgot you were a monster. Ya certainly was last night." She laughs again and waits for me to take the next turn in the conversation. I don't want to. She called me, but only to give me the chance to make the next move. She'll have to do it, though. I'm satiated for the moment. "Are you still there? Hello?"

"Yeah."

"Oh, I was wondering if ya wanted to come over tonight after bar close. I don't work tomorrow at all."

"Sure."

"You don't have to work, right? I thought you might have a set tonight."

"Nope. I don't know. What is today?" Last night was my last night at the Whistle Stop Station. My agent has me set up to work a show at UW-Whitewater on Saturday night. "Wednesday. No."

"Okay, then. Come, if that's okay?"

"Yes." I enjoy not caring if this goes well or not. At first, I was having trouble talking and keeping the phone to my ear, but it's getting easier. "Listen, I got to go. But I'll see you tonight."

"Ya, okay." Her voice is soft and timid through the phone. I don't want that from her. "Wait, let me give you my number in case you can't make it, okay? It's 651-603-7260."

"Got it," I say and hang up.

The phone immediately rings, and I grab it in frustration.

"I didn't get the joke, Mikey." Alaine sounds only a little irritated, and this disappoints me,

"Me either."

"If you don't want to talk about what's bothering you, that's fine. I take the hint. You have a little trouble using the phone when you wake up in the middle of the afternoon. But let's do something. We have to spend some time together before you go back on the road."

It seems like I have left her far behind- yesterday was a lifetime ago. But because of that, I can see she doesn't care what is going on with me. She wants me to keep her company and entertain her. A bizarre and uncomfortable scene of Janet and Alaine together spins in my head. Alaine wouldn't know what to make of her.

"You know what," I say, winding up into aggressive comments but then stop. This is my chance to show her my new found independence. I cannot separate this thought from the whirligig maelstrom that is now my mind. "We should get together. Why don't you and Dan and Janet and me go out to dinner tomorrow night?" My voice comes out upbeat. "Yeah, you, me, them. We'll do a reenactment of The Last Supper."

On Alaine's end of the phone, a door latch clicks, and a moment later, glass bottles tinkle as a refrigerator door opens. Alaine is on her cell phone in the breakroom at work. The door shuts again. Perhaps she was waiting for privacy, but it is several more moments before she speaks. "I guess that sounds good."

It makes me smile to hear how hurt she sounds that I won't be her personal clown. "Let me call Janet."

I click the phone and hear nothing. I slam the receiver into the base and then pull them apart. Shit. What am I doing? Finally, the phone gives me a dial tone. A man answers when I guess the numbers Janet gave me. After a few more tries, a woman's voice answers. "Janet?"

"No, there's no Janet here."

I almost allow regret to happen. Phone numbers were one of those things I was not going to hold on to in my mind. And writing it down was caring what happened. Luckily, on the next attempt, Janet answers. "Hello." Does luck replace regret if you let it?

"Hi, it's me."

"Oh. Ya, you about missed me. I was out the door to go to work."

"Yeah? Well, I was wondering if you want to go out to dinner with some friends of mine tomorrow night."

"Ya bet. Are you going to be there, too?"

"What?" I do not understand that at all.

"It's a joke. As a comedian, I thought you might like that one," she says with a fruity laugh.

"I am not a comedian." I reverse the Elephant Man quote in a strained voice. "I am an animal."

She laughs. "Okay, so are we going to do this? Tomorrow, eh? We can meet at the restaurant or your apartment."

"I'll pick you up," I say, realizing it's an hour's drive each way. But she can't be in my apartment, and for full effect, I want to walk into the restaurant with her on my arm. I think for a moment of her perched on my arm like a pirate's parrot, and it makes me chuckle.

15

Janet's Firebird rumbles down the freeway. The throttle responds to my slightest pressure on the gas pedal and allows me to pass people with a quick jerk of the steering wheel. I'm driving recklessly to recreate the adrenaline rush of yesterday. Whether I was ruining my career or pressing my groin into hers, it felt good not to care.

"Mikey?"

I turn to Janet. "What?"

"Are you okay? Ya were saying how my car is a classic, and I shouldn't put a lot of miles on it, and then you stopped in mid-sentence for like ten minutes."

She is exaggerating. "I must have gotten distracted by the traffic."

Janet flips through her CDs in their square carrying case. "Goin' on the highway is good for the old girl," she says. "It'll blow the carbon out."

It had been her idea to take her car. Her handing me the keys comes to me as distant as a childhood memory. "Do you always let guys you just met have a crack at her?" I chuckle at my little sexual innuendo.

"Umm," she says, serious. "No. Not always for guys at all. This is kind of a new thing for me. Usually, I talk the talk, but when it comes time to go beyond talking, I'm all bluff." She studies her disks.

"But not anymore. I was in this long relationship. The whole time I was his nursemaid, babysitter, and bank account out of a sense of obligation. So, my new motto is if it's crazy, do it. Is that your new motto, too, Mikey? The last time you worked Whistle Stop Station, you were engaged, but I think that's over for you."

I remember the shows at the Whistle Stop Station last year. But not Janet being on staff. How could I have not noticed a woman that attracts constant glances from men? I was wrapped up in Karen. Like a moron. "This has a 350 in it?"

"The 400. Four-barrel. The bigger engine costs a lot more in insurance, though." Janet tucks the burning cigarette she had in her hand into her mouth so that she can slide a CD into the stereo with her long, red nails squeezing it.

"What's that you're putting in?" I change the subject because my interest in engines and bad relationships are exhausted.

She yells, "Aerosmith" the same instant Steven Tyler's voice explodes through the speakers and fills the car. She yells along to the first verse.

"I used to be a Green Day fanatic," she says. "But that's cuz I was in love with Billie Joe."

The speed limit goes from 65 to 55, and the traffic gets heavier. "These people, Dan and Alaine. They're a little put-offish." I've decided to tell her this to absolve myself if she has a terrible time.

"Listen," Janet says, finally turning the music down. "Why are we doing this? Introducing me to your friends. Alaine isn't an ex-girlfriend or something?"

I squint forward. "I always wanted a car with a hood scoop." But the guys in high school who thought they were hot shit had muscle cars. Another thing I'm no longer interested in. "No."

"Then I'm like the first woman after a bad break-up, and they're going to be a crutch."

"More like an obligation. I needed to go to dinner with these two.

I wanted to at least buy you dinner. An evening was born." Her accusation makes me grip the steering wheel. "But yeah, you are the first woman after a bad break-up. In case they bring it up."

She looks at me out of the corner of her eye. "Do you want to tell me about what happened to you and your fiancé?"

"Do you want to tell me more about your last boyfriend?"

"No."

"Okay, then." I smile, impressed to have sized her up while still feverish. "In a way, though, this is to show them everything's fine with me. I am using you, okay?"

"At least you're buying me dinner first."

I pull off on our exit, taking the curve at sixty and making the tires squeal. Part of me simply wants to be having dinner with Alaine. "So tonight, I got to be human. Then it's right back to crazy, okay?"

She leans down and blows her hot breath through my pants, and puts her teeth on my dick. When she sits back up, she has a smile on her face, and her tight, blue dress shifts to expose her cleavage in a black bra. The old Mikey would have felt shame for copping a look, so I cup her breast.

16

Janet tells me as we make our way to the table that she has been to Ciatti's a couple of times. This was Karen's favorite restaurant. I select a response to Janet that sounds reasonable and calm. "I've never been here, but people say it's nice. Dan picked it out."

As soon as the hostess hands us our menus, our waitress comes up and asks us if we would like something to drink. I have not made introductions yet and let the waitress prolong it. Alaine asks for a Margarita, Dan orders a Gibson. I order a beer and respond I don't care when the waitress questions what kind. Janet fills in, "Bring two Budweiser."

"Make it a pitcher," I say. I will become an alcoholic to have a repeat of last night. To be uninhibited and unencumbered. To last so long and have this skittish energy that's getting stronger by the minute.

Janet extends her hand. "I'm Janet Juscinsky," she says in her warm, harsh Minnesotan voice.

I mumble, "This is Alaine and Dan. Alaine, Dan, this is Janet."

"Mikey has trouble with social conventions," Alaine says, taking her hand before Dan shakes it. "Hi there."

"I was waiting for the damn waitress. It's not like none of us doesn't know what is going on here." Alaine's sideways glance gets me more agitated, so I laugh to cover my anger. "A nice dinner."

The main headings are incomprehensible, and the words Spaghetti, Vitello-Veal, and Pollo-Chicken sickens me. It makes me feel the roundness of my gut and how it lays on my belt, and the fold where my rib cage ends and my gut bulges out like the Metrodome.

"You look tired, Mikey," Alaine says.

"We were up until five A.M." I glance at Janet. She smirks at me with raised eyebrows.

Then Janet lays her menu down. "I'm going to have the Baked Ziti." A common order.

Alaine doesn't quite look up from her menu. "You'll like that. It's good here. In fact, I think that is what Mikey and I ordered the first time we ate at Ciatti's."

"I guess I was here before." These are all the words I can give her as an apology. This is a quiet restaurant, but everything seems loud and grating. The waitress is talking a couple of tables away. A busser bangs through the kitchen door with a bus tub. The light over the table. These three people are making me breathe hard.

We order when the waitress comes with our drinks. Dan gets the Vitello Parmigiana, and Alaine gets the Pollo Florentine. "Chef's Salad," I say last, anticipating the cool strips of ham and turkey. The waitress writes it down. "French dressing."

"Did you go on a diet?" Alaine asks.

"Should I be on one?" Salads never fill me up, but it will not be warm or taste of garlic.

The spinning of my mind is making me sick to my stomach. I want the soothing redness of the French dressing.

"I'm just asking if that's all you want. You love Italian food and can get a salad anywhere. Get something you like."

"If it's good enough for Santa Claus, it's good enough for me."

Dan, reading the table tent advertising the drink specials, glances at me. "Since when does Santa Claus eat salad?"

"I meant the other holiday imaginary creature that isn't Jesus. The big rabbit that brings chocolate. If it's good enough for Peter Cottontail."

"Are you okay?" Alaine asks me.

Janet needs to be brought into the conversation. She hasn't said anything since I admitted my lie. "Janet, do you want an appetizer?"

"No, I don't really eat a lot."

Dan stirs his drink. "So Janet, you live in Saint Cloud?"

"You betcha. All my life." Janet touches her fingertip to the foam in her beer. "I lived in the U of M dorms before dropping out – well, only one semester, so that doesn't count."

"Oh, really." Alaine sounds incredulous at the fact that Janet went to school. "What did you major in?"

Janet laughs. "You can't say you majored in something when you only go half a year, eh? I thought maybe psychology. I didn't want something general like history."

"Or English," Dan says.

"We both majored in English." Alaine smiles and looks at Dan.

"God, I'm sorry."

"He's teasing."

"But you aren't wrong," Dan says, and I remember why I hate him. These three people are making me sick. "We both had an emphasis on advertising. Otherwise, an English major won't get you anywhere in this world."

"That's what I meant. One waitress I work with has a degree in history. She's like me. She could never teach, so what's she going to do with that?" Janet hee-hees. "Where do you two work?"

Janet is about to get buried with things she knows nothing about. She is here to make Alaine and Dan interact with a lowbrow bartender. That's why I wanted this. But I didn't think about Janet being overwhelmed. We are sitting at a small table with Dan across from me and Alaine across from Janet. I reach over and put my hand on Janet's nyloned leg for a moment to let her know she's doing okay. But touching her, I flash to how she looked when she came to the door in her sleeveless dress. The neckline exposed her chest, but no cleavage. Still, the fabric stretched tight and melded her breasts into a steep Indian mound on the terrain of her torso. Her dress tightened around her stomach, ruining the smoothness of the dress in an exciting way. She had her hair moussed out and cupped around dangling earrings. Before we left, she pinched the bottom of her dress around her thighs and pulled it back down from riding up. I never even had a chance before with a girl that wears tight dresses. The thought of it riding up and her leaving it that way makes me squeeze her leg a little further up.

Janet smiles as she turns toward me.

"You are so quiet tonight, Mikey," Alaine says. I know she is wondering what our private joke is

"I work for Planned Parenthood," Dan says. "Officially, I work for the Public Relations Department, but I do a lot of work developing an administrative LAN platform for their computer network. Alaine is the creative director at Artifacts Advertising Studio. Her English major got her a job as a copywriter, and she worked up from there."

"You all met in college, eh?" Janet takes a long swallow of her beer.

Dan answers, "Alaine and I had classes together. She switched her major to English junior year. We were assigned to the same group to develop a television ad campaign."

"Before that, she was an art major," I say. "She's really talented. And she didn't switch majors until after she was dating you."

Alaine laughs and stretches her hand along the table toward Janet. "I was going to be this great suffering artist but grew out of it. Too many artists wallow around in self-pity and drugs." She adjusts her drink on the table. "Still, I like to show the guys at work. I can still come up with some interesting designs."

She works in the art room whenever her job lets her. I don't mention this. This was the heart of my Alaine, not this Alaine plotting with Dan and Janet to make me a fool. Spite makes me say something I've said a thousand times as an encouragement. "You should still paint when you get a chance. On the weekends."

"All my computer stuff is jammed into the spare bedroom," Dan says before Alaine can say anything. He wants to tell his version of the story. They will wait until they build a house, and then Dan will build her a studio with the perfect light. But this will not happen because Dan will always keep her away from painting. His little logical, jealous mind can't handle it.

The waitress comes and sets the food in front of us. The others all announce how good their meals look. Because Dan chose this restaurant, he goes on with bragging about the food. I feel myself getting farther and farther away from them. The human interactions are distant sounds. I concentrate only on my fork piercing the lettuce and waiting for the last of the salad to be gone.

"So," Dan says. "Can you get us free drinks if we go to Whistle Stop Station?"

His rude question brings me back. I ask, "What?" But I say it so light that no one hears it or acknowledges it.

Janet gives him a sideways smile. Her bartender smirk, "Actually, the management watches us pretty close unless you came on a Sunday night."

There is nothing I can impress Alaine with about Janet except her looks. Janet looks like a circus performer next to Alaine. Alaine has prepared for the air-conditioned air with an olive-green sweater with one button in the front and sleeves that come half past her elbows over a lighter green blouse. It leaves her delicate wrists bare to make you want to hold her hand. She is eating a small piece of chicken, efficient, sweet. This makes me put my hand on Janet's back. Alaine looks at me, and I realize my face is stoic. It shows no signs of the affection my hand is giving.

Now Dan gives Janet a smirk. "I was kidding again. You know, in college, our goal was to find a way to get free beer. Janet, how was your ziti? Lainey, how about your Pollo Florentine? My Vitello Parmigiana was delicious."

He got some very goods from the girls—score one for you, Dan.

"Some of the other Ciatti's were sold off and franchised out," he keeps on. "That's why I only go to this one. It's still under the same management."

"Yeah, I know," Janet says. "I've worked at a few restaurants where they got sold, and the new owners think they have to change everything where we're doing things a good way already. Plus, they go skimpy on things to get back some of the money they paid for the place."

"Mikey, how was your show the other night?" Alaine asks.

"It was wild," Janet answers, looking at me. "He was running all over, breaking stuff. He had the crowd going wild."

For a moment, Alaine looks confused. "What? That's not your act, and you didn't even mention that to me yesterday. Something is wrong. Even tonight."

I slam my beer glass down. Janet and I have finished the pitcher. Saying that in front of Dan and Janet angers me. More and more, I feel like I did onstage – unable to think and incapable of controlling my next behavior.

"His show was exciting," Janet says to defend me.

The waitress slides the bill on the table. By the time I free my wallet from my pants, Dan has his credit card out and folds it into the black book. The proper response in this game is to drag our interactions out by offering him money. The words won't form in my mouth. Let him think I'm cheap.

We all stand to leave. "I think you two were rude to ask Janet to supply you with free drinks and to talk about your guys' big, important jobs." I lay a twenty on the table for the waitress, like Janet, who is dependent on tips, and walk away from Dan and Alaine.

As soon as I jackrabbit the car out of the parking lot, Janet says, "I asked them about their jobs. Thanks for defending me, but I wasn't made to feel embarrassed, I don't think."

17

My duffel bag is on the seat next to me, my clothes stuffed in, the zipper unzipped. A road comic needs a system for packing. My well-developed one has become as incomprehensible as second-hand advice, and I have taken random items from my apartment. I didn't leave Janet's until after she left to work the lunch rush and only after I masturbated into a pair of her panties and threw them away.

The moment I got into my apartment, my brain attacked me. It slammed me with so many thoughts I couldn't get a handle on any. My gig in Wisconsin is not until tomorrow, but I wanted to pack, and after I packed, I slung my duffel bag over my shoulder. On the road, Alaine can't come to see me. She knows my cell phone plan has only enough minutes for emergencies.

My body reacts to pressing the accelerator down like it is physically sprinting. But I have already been driving recklessly. The car lurches and tilts back slightly with an increase in speed. I slow down and then speed up to hear the carburetor gasp for more air to feed the eight cylinders in their wasteful frenzy. The rusted muffler growls

I-94 is busy, and I'm passing people on the right and left,

increasing speed to watch myself pass them. The speed limit on the bridge over the St Croix is fifty-five, so I slow down with the traffic. The wheels whine over the steel grids and hum as they hit the cement freeway on the Wisconsin side.

My lit cigarette sits in the ashtray and burns without me wanting to inhale it. I think it must be the after-effects of being sick, but I haven't finished a cigarette in days.

A sign telling me the distance to Madison makes me think of the time Alaine, Karen, and I took I-94 down to Madison for Halloween weekend. Each sign will remind me of the three of us sitting in the front seat with Karen next to me as we drank and waved at everyone we passed. We kept stopping to go pee.

This was just before Karen and I started going out and after my stunt at the Veterinary school. Since I surprised her in the examination room, we called each other every night. She smiled when she caught me looking at her, but I couldn't bring myself to believe she liked me. I was sure I had missed the signals. She just wanted to be friends. At one point on Halloween, Karen and I were alone outside a bar. It was chilly, and her nose and cheeks were red. We were toe to toe. Any other man would have made his move, but I didn't. I stood there and kept talking, wanting to stroke her red cheeks.

Those are not my memories. I twist the radio on and try to listen to Vanessa Williams singing on the radio. Instantly I know I will not be able to stand any music and turn the radio back off.

The last time I rode with Karen pushes into my silent head. She waited in the no parking zone of the Animal Science building in her blue parka. We were supposed to go talk things out. The only thing I cared about was not losing her, but she kept saying things so incredulous that I found myself fighting back. We went to Mounds Park to talk without people walking by, but she had already said everything before we got there. As I babbled in desperation to say the right thing, she faced her window and cried. "Take me home," she said after a long silence between us.

"I love you," I had said, pulling in front of her apartment. She turned to me and looked with her eyes moist and red.

I twist the radio back on as loud as it will go. Distortion and static blasts until I twist the knob to the oldies station. "There she was just a walking down the street singing 'Do wa diddy dum diddy dum,'" I yowl. "Before I knew she was walking next to me singing, 'Do wah diddy dum diddy do. Well, she looked good, looked good. Looked fine, looked fine. Looked good. Looked fine, and I nearly lost my mind'."

My singing breaks into cursing and banging on the steering wheel. Finally, I growl. When I am quiet and have turned the radio off, last night with Janet comes into my head. Then Janet just standing behind a bar. This dissolves into a flash, and all the women that have made a fool of me sit on lawn chairs in my head. The girls I had a crush on in high school, my first girlfriend, Karen, Alaine, and my mother, are sitting there talking about me. Then they aren't sitting on lawn chairs, but on furniture you would find in a waiting room.

A horn blares as I have drifted into the left lane and almost hit a passing car. I jerk the car back into the right lane without knowing if it's safe. My heart is pounding, but the only thing that scares me is how real those women seemed.

Fifteen minutes out of Eau Claire, I pull off the freeway to buy a six-pack of beer. The guy at the register tries to make small talk, but I don't even acknowledge his presence. I put money down on the counter. If I had tried to speak, it would have just come out as a snarl.

The convenience store and a road leading into a small town are the only things around me, but I have a hard time finding my way back on the freeway.

A hole in the exhaust manifold ticks when I accelerate. Mile after mile, I let it, and the brash light through the windshield overwhelm my senses. The warm air rushing through the open windows and the harsh beer down my throat makes me sweat. My body aches from being too much weight in the worn-out seat.

The speedometer says seventy-five, but I can't think of what the speed limit is. Is a cop watching me as I twist to get comfortable and roll my window up and down? Did another driver report that I am drinking beer? These questions try to scare me. I have another conversation with myself. You had to leave this morning. Because you were thinking about her. You thought about her the whole time you were having sex with Janet.

Right now, running away is seeding her into my thoughts. But away from everybody, I can make my transformation complete. Then those memories won't be mine, and I can escape the anger Karen causes.

18

At a rest stop, too many of the drivers that taunted me as I sat like a circus animal in the cage of my car are pulling in as well. I escape the idling engines by going into a small nature area with a wood chip path.

The hum of the freeway traffic goes on, but the wooded area is empty. No one else wants to be ten minutes later to their destination. I walk off the path and soak some ferns. Tall, straight trees canopy the wood chip path and the small white flowers growing in the underlying detritus. There must be small animals that live at this wayside, this toilet area. It is cool in here and peaceful, with the sun mingling with fluttering leaves.

It is serene, even with the whirr of wheels on cement. I can't be back among them or get back onto the giant needle that will inject me at sixty-five miles an hour into Madison. Whitewater is south of Madison, but the idea of zooming urbanites and the young grungy college students distress me. I can't think of State Street with all kinds of people, even the freaks, living their lives in a way I never could. As they want to.

Cutting perpendicular to the path, I walk to a fence, the deepest part of this area. I pull my pants and underpants down. Then I yank the two shirts I'm wearing over my head. My cheap canvas shoes come off next so I can free myself of clothes. The debris of the ground and the new seedlings sprouting randomly call me to plant myself.

My feet tense up to feel the fallen branches and the wet, cool dirt, and I realize I am acting impulsively. These trees are peaceful, but I want to escape without peace.

Only continuing on will allow me to strip away everything that isn't animal instinct. This thought makes me put my clothes back on. Out here, I will get nothing, and I am tired of getting nothing.

It gets brighter and warmer as the covering of trees opens up, and I walk toward the strangers getting in and out of their vehicles. It's like coming out of the "It's a Small World Ride" at Disneyland and into a fist fight. A family with three kids passes me as they go check out the nature trail. I get back into the car and get back onto the freeway.

19

Mikey is still in the woods, stripped off me and out of me. What Mikey wanted still stings. I know his story and his memories, but they do not haunt me.

MIKEY'S PAST

Mikey slid his hand over Karen's sweater to pull her close. During the week, they made out in stolen moments when her roommates abandoned the living room. They had long goodbyes in the car after a movie. It was only Sunday nights after Karen had gotten all her weekend studying done that they indulged in the pressure of their two bodies together on his bed.

She reached up to put her fingers through his hair, and his hand slid down to touch the resulting exposed skin of her lower back. His hand hit a ridge of crumpled denim. He explored it, puzzled until realizing her jeans were unbuttoned and unzipped. At first, he moved his hand to her butt. When she drew her leg up onto him, he slid his hand to the crook of her knee. With any other woman, he would have felt awkward to be able to reach his long arm the entire length of her body.

Her crotch against his with her open jeans and her tense muscles told him she felt the same urge to press their bodies closer. Her cool, thin hands went up under his shirt and along his bare back. She pulled up on his shirt. Without thinking of it, Mikey lifted his body up so that the shirt responded to her tugging faster. The shirt was up across his chest. He sat up and yanked it over his head. At the same time, Karen took her sweater off. In the low light coming in from the street, Mikey gazed at her soft skin rising up out of the darkness of the denim. He outright ogled her breasts in a white bra. He did not know what was going to happen, but he did not want to ruin the mood. His eyes snapped to her face. Karen was looking away. They kissed, and she unbuttoned his jeans. Lying down together, he pulled her unbuttoned jeans past her hips.

This was all new. In the recent weeks, they had wallowed in the ecstasy of heavy petting without wanting to make their love and desire less spiritual. They held each other and whispered their closely guarded thoughts. Only in the darkness did she talk about being nine and the beginning of her belief she would never be good enough. Her dad grounded her for getting a B on her report card. Only in the darkness, she talked of growing up trying to impress her parents, but the great was expected and her mistakes disappointing. She talked – saying it aloud for the first time – of trying to be exactly what her boyfriends wanted until him. Because they had been friends, Mikey knew the true her and liked her as she was.

Mikey told her things he had been waiting his whole life to say. This was why he never tried to go beyond petting. He was ready for her to be his first sexual partner, but she was already the first to make him feel worthy. That was more than enough. He told her about growing up with it just being him and his mom until she decided a two-person family was not enough. In response, Karen gave him the words he took as a gift. "Tell me, Mikey. I want to know."

They rubbed against each other. He placed his hands on her

undulating hip. Just to attune himself to the frequency of her movements. This induced the not unfamiliar urge to enter her, but he only realized they would not stop when he slipped his hand into her underwear, and she moaned into his ear. Together they would let desire carry them away and see, finally, where they could go. He had her bra off, feeling her breasts against him, touching them with his fingertips, his eyes only on her face.

She twisted herself from their embrace and leaned down to her purse on the floor. Something told him not to ask her what she was doing. The words wanted to come out, but he knew what she was getting. When she placed the condom in front of her soft, rolling belly, he picked it up.

"Do you want to do this?" he asked.

"You don't?"

"God, yes." He kissed her. "Be patient, though, okay?"

"We have to be patient with each other."

Mike fumbled to get it out of the package. What if the condom was too big? What if he came putting it on?

He laid down and applied the condom. He did his best not to hurry but soon found himself rolling onto her. Holding himself up on both hands, he moved his pelvis to find her vagina. Then she gently took him and guided him inside her. Her warmth and smoothness enveloped him. He wanted to keep still and just experience this world but began to move back and forth.

Every movement was a struggle not to come, and he came quickly. He lowered himself beside her, his head next to her with his back arched as he withdrew. She kissed his ear lobe and moaned. "I love you, Mikey."

Out of breath, he kissed her. "I'll get better."

"See, sex is not that big of a deal." Later and much later, he cringed thinking about her saying that, but at the time, he thought she meant they were so much more than physical. She laid her head on his chest.

"I feel so safe with you," she said, with her eyes closed.

20

Highway 89 becomes Main Street in Whitewater, and this takes me to the University. I miss the street the auditorium is on and go around the block to get on Prince Street. There is no traffic, and the wide sidewalks are bare except for an occasional student. At a stop light, a girl in a short skirt with tan legs crosses in front of the car. With her is a boy her own age. His shoulders are broad- not as broad as mine, but with tight muscles, because he works out. Another girl walks alone with a bandana on her head and a peasant skirt. College campuses draw men to drive by them with the promise of young women. But school's out for the summer, and there isn't much bare skin on display. Usually, though, men are in luck. Wisconsin college girls start wearing skirts before the end of February.

Up Prince Street is the Irwin Something Auditorium. I pull into the parking lot to see the front of it. It's a white building with large high windows and large trees surrounding it. I've played in all kinds of auditoriums, but the ones on college campuses always try harder to be stately. In front of the brick building, a portable sign with plastic letters reads:

Alpha Beta Gamma's
Benefit for Chris Danforth
Featuring Comedians:
Richard Bernstein
And
The Animal
July 15th
7:30

A truck forces me to stop reading the sign and go. The Hamilton House sign appears, and I have to turn into the parking lot without throwing my blinker on.

* * *

"This is Mike Haskell. I want to talk to him." My agent's secretary tells me one moment, please.

I have to wait four minutes before Larry's brittle voice comes on. "Mikey, it's good to finally hear from you."

"Do you know what they are calling me in this shit town?"

"Where are you? In Wisconsin already?"

"Answer the question, Larry."

"Yeah," he says. "The Animal. I worked pretty fast."

"Where the fuck did you get that from?"

"From your act." I picture him now in his small, paneled office. Both elbows on his metal desk, a cigarette in his ceramic ashtray, and his butt hanging out his swivel chair. "You haven't returned my phone calls."

"Fuck you and your giant ashtray," I say. Larry is the nicest guy you'd ever want to meet, and I had my phone off.

"Mikey, what are you pissed about? I got a call from Don from the Whistle Stop Station. He starts off by telling me, 'Luckily, the customers liked his new act.' But then he goes on about you upsetting a customer and that you should have checked with him first before doing those things." Larry shows his weakness by hesitating. I scratch my face with the receiver until he realizes I want him to get to the punch line.

"So I am sitting there not knowing what he is talking about. He is telling me about you doing wild things and looking terrible. You were a hit, though. I really did try to get a hold of you to find out what's going on, but if this is your new act, I had to call Center Net in time for them to promote it. From what Don said, I can promote your new act all over the country. You will be thanking me because once I get this promoted, you will play the big clubs on both coasts."

I want this conversation over. "Sure."

"So, why are you calling me, then? And why didn't you tell me about the new act?"

21

On the road, a smoker's first venture out is for cigarettes. But I'm walking away from the hotel only to get out of the room. Animals don't smoke, I think, and it makes me laugh. It means I'm transforming and getting further away from myself. Mikey, the comedian, is a mere vestigial structure.

There will be no thrills in Whitewater, Wisconsin, but what exciting thing is in the big cities? Bars? You need a group of friends to have fun there or anywhere. Nightclubs are exciting if you are young and drunk enough to do stupid things. Even then, it's nothing a different location can't provide. Even then, the event doesn't live up to what you thought the experience would be, and neither is the person you came with. Working in the big cities, I still wasted as much time as possible in the hotel room.

This is not an aimless walk. Craving for more beer punctuates each thought, and I must attend to it. I got drunk when I was who I was, and there are stories to tell. But even in college, Mikey always had more fun waiting to go out to the bars. His favorite part of the night was eating breakfast at Perkins or Country Kitchen. When Mikey was drunk, he was himself. Quiet, knowing the next word out of his mouth would come out wrong. So he didn't drink usually. Mikey got high on his persona, his reputation to be fun. He would be excited and confident from having his friends laugh. Then he could go off on any subject, making jokes. Mikey, the comedian, could talk to anyone. He would see drinking as a sign my transformation is wrong. I embrace the wrong,

Karen fell in love with Mikey, the Comedian. She must have been so disappointed when his magic failed, and she pulled back the curtain.

Mikey stayed sober so that he loosened up. In one of his journals, he has written this into a joke, but I can't perform it. I can perform nothing.

Walk. Concentrate on movement. Stalk. My feet slap the sidewalk. Frizzy hair tickles my ears and makes me shrug my shoulders. I stink from being in the hot car all day.

Blocks from the college is a neighborhood bar, and I go in. There is no loud music, just a TV over the bar with a baseball game on. There are seven guys, including the bartender, sitting in front of the TV. They are in the back of this long, narrow room.

I walk on the hardwood floor and sit at the other end of the bar, away from the men and the TV. The bartender lets me sit a while.

"Can of Miller," I say when the bartender does come over. I barely get the words out and set money on the bar, so I don't have to talk again.

With alcohol gurgling down my throat, I can feel the metamorphosis become more complete. The animal becomes stronger. It forgets stupid thoughts.

I slam the beer and get another. The bartender has set a glass next to the beer, but I do not use it. The craving remains, but I feel stronger having fed it, so I look over at the men. This is their bar, and they do not want anyone else in it—especially someone like me. They give me the stink eye and make comments. The bartender sees that my beer is gone but does not budge. They reject me. I pick up the glass and hold it.

If you want to throw it, throw it. The glass hits the wall filled with plaques from pool tournaments and dart leagues behind the men.

"What the fuck," the bartender says, and his buddies slide off their bar stools and stand up. Because they swivel the backed stools to get off them, they don't intimidate me.

"That's what you get for serving him," one of them says.

"You got a problem here, freak," another says. This one has his jeans pulled up on an immense beer belly.

"How is Sue and the kids?" I ask him. "You guys should have one more and try for a girl." I stand up, feeling my height. There is one man whose rail-thin and a man in his sixties, a father of one of the other men, I would bet, but the rest of them are a good size. The bartender looks to be in his early twenties and must work out. These men probably were in a lot of fights in high school, but now they are family men with two-car garages to go home to. They do not have me cornered, so I will not pounce like every muscle in my body tells me to. I shove the screen door to the place open and leave.

The houses as I walk further along become small businesses in old wooden buildings. A rusty barber pole is bolted to one building. Next to it is a shop with dusty vacuum cleaners in the window. The pawn shop next to that is closed but has a neon open sign lit up. On the corner is another bar, and I look in the propped-open door. There is a middle-aged woman bartender, a man in a flannel shirt with the sleeves cut off, and two older women in blouses.

At dusk, I peer into another bar to see if I can get off my feet for a while. It is too much like the others. Funny how bars have become my destination.

In the older part of the city, the lawns are small, and the streets are not curbed. I believe more people are desperate here and will lower themselves further into desperation as they try to escape it with alcohol and drugs. This is where my craving can be satiated.

Here I will find the kind of bar Mikey was terrified of. The kind of bar where someone like me won't inflict himself on good people.

On Alaine. On Janet even. I welcomed the Janet that let me fuck her without even knowing her last name. But the Janet that called me the next day had a voice too vulnerable; too I want to get to know you better.

A little further along, I turn onto a long thoroughfare and begin to pass a gray rotting structure that leans in on itself. It has a row of large sliding doors for loading trucks. After the building is a one-story bar with a sign faded black. There are two picture windows on either side of the dented steel door, but these windows are blackened except for a space to show neon beer signs. Miller High Life and Bud Light. Maintaining my pace, I slide into the bar.

It is crowded and dark. Quiet despite the bar being fairly full. The stench of stale smoke and beer hits me. There is also the smell of must or mildew—the smell of an old building. The floor is scuffed up with black and white checkerboard tile. It doesn't fit with the atmosphere. The red, cushioned booths and western-style wooden chairs seem out of place, too.

The bartender stands in front of me. I glance down the scarred surface of the bar to see mostly Old Style cans. That's what I get, hoping to blend in.

The bartender looks at me over his big bifocal glasses and slips the two dollars from my money on the bar. Though he is not smiling, his mouth is open, and his big white false teeth make his face look like a decaying skull. It is a moment before he pulls a can from the refrigerator below and gives me ample time to size up this study in aging biker. He is at least fifty with gray hair in a ponytail, with a leather vest over a Big Johnson T-shirt.

The beer goes down hard. I always hated Old Style, but slam it and order another one. The guy next to me is leaning back from the bar with his head cupped in his hands. Every few seconds, he convulses into a hiccup. The bartender takes the guy's empty glass and replaces it with a new glass of whiskey. The drunk reaches for it and takes a drink.

The jukebox clicks on, and "Welcome to the Jungle" by Guns

and Roses crashes out of the speakers. I perceive that these rough-looking people might take more offense to someone different being near them than the men at the other bar. My neck muscles tighten—every moment, I expect the bartender to grab me by the back of the neck and spin me around.

I lean my head back and close my eyes in anticipation. When I open my eyes, a few people are taking glances at me. But then, many people would gawk at a six-foot-six thing covered in fur. The men in this bar have their leather jackets or vests on. Their village people's costume is complete with black boots and multiple tattoos. The women are the same, except for one.

A slender girl sits at one of the tables up on a platform in the corner. She looks under eighteen, but the guy she is with is at least thirty-five. Maybe she only looks young. She has a small, skinny face with big eyes surrounded by a large amount of black mascara.

Her guy is less than five foot six and thin in a hard way. He has long, flyaway hair and a groomed beard. While this pretty girl is tucked up under his arm, he is deep in a conversation with the other guy at the table. His hand at the end of the arm draped over her flops around like a dying fish as he talks. The other guy has a large, round face and long greasy hair.

His girl is the only thing worth looking at in the bar. Yet, I try to avoid trouble by reading the notes taped to the cash register. Do not take checks from... Use the "Specials" key for happy hour. Turn key to z and hit total to total out register. Fear God, but remember I sign your paychecks.

I turn around and watch the girl again out of spite. God has sent me a literal sign to fear Him. Her guy keeps talking to the moron across from him and ignores her. She is wearing a blue Reebok shirt of thin material with a hood. Her straight hair brushes the hood as it lays crumpled on her shoulders. I think of caressing her neck and having her hair run across the top of my hand.

This girl catches me watching her. She must be used to getting leered at—especially where the other women are rough, hard-looking, and older. Men put on shit-eating manners for young, good-looking girls. Perhaps her body is turned toward me because I am new. The other reason, perhaps, is that I can compete with the other shit-eaters now. The why doesn't matter.

Without taking my eyes off her, I lift the can of beer to drink. My head already pounds painlessly from the alcohol, but I guzzle what is left and buy two shots of Jack Daniels. I want to impress the girl. Her guy is still just talking to his friend.

The guy grabs her head that has been pointed at me too long, shakes it. His mouth snarls something. The girl cringes, and I stand up.

He pushes her out of the booth and gets up. She is something he steps over before weaving through the tables to get to me. I still tower above him when he gets in my face.

"I'm going to beat your ass in," he says.

I lash out but only seem to touch him. His first punch is to my jaw. My head doesn't register what is happening, and I fall back to the bar. I stand up, so I tower over him. The booze and not eating today has made me weak. I may fall down before he hits me again. I swing at him. Miss. He hits me in the gut. The pain goes through my torso like shock waves. So does rage.

Without planning, I hit him back and keep swinging. The hits do not go where I want them to, and most glance off without full force, but my arms ache to move. He is hitting me, too, but I can't feel it. With both hands together, I hit him in the chest and then bring them down on his head. His body staggers under my hands. I shove him against a wall and bring my forearm to his face, knocking his head into a frosted Jack Daniel's mirror. Both fall to the floor.

My whole body shakes with a desire to keep hitting him. The bartender is holding his fat friend and yelling at him to put the knife away.

Everyone is up to see the fight, but I push through them to get the girl. I grab her arm and say, "Time to go.".

22

I walk fast and do not turn around until the bar is no longer visible. The girl is six steps behind me.

"You go on the Jay and Tim show, don't you?" she asks.

I look at her.

"Your picture is on their website."

The radio show, it dawns on me. I do their show when I'm in Indianapolis. Whenever Tim makes fun of Jay only being five foot five, he brings up pictures taken of me and Jay standing together. "Check out our website, folks, and see Jay standing next to the sequoia named Mikey Haskell."

"I live with him," she says then.

On the way to my hotel, she talks about the guy. His name is Jesse. "He cheats on me. But to tell you the truth, I'm bored with him, too. I need excitement. You know?"

I need her to shut up.

"He doesn't think twice about how he treats me. Well, he's going to think twice now." She is walking fast. The wind blows against her so that her clinging shirt defines small breasts and an athletic body.

She is wearing shiny gray workout pants with a white stripe down each leg. "You don't talk much, do you?"

I'm dizzy from the beer and Jesse's punches and from being in the middle of not knowing what I am doing. Across the street is my hotel. Somehow, we've been close to it the whole time. "Here we go."

"Do you have a car? I got a real kinky spot." Her saying this pisses me off, but I nod and pull my keys out of my pocket.

"I thought you'd have a badass car," she says, getting in.

We drive farther down Main Street until she points. "Turn left here." She pulls her arms into her shirt and undoes her bra. Then with her bra in one hand, she shoves her arms back through the armholes. She flings the bra onto the dashboard and pulls her shoes off. "Here." She points with a smirk. It's a church.

She has me pull into the circle drive, so we are in front of the double doors. The bell tower stands above us, wide and brick. A spotlight on the lawn illuminates a sign with the mass schedule times. "Isn't this fucking crazy?"

I put my hand under her shirt and cup her breast. My senses come alive with the smell of her perfume and alcohol and cigarettes. My own smell is sweat. The crickets chirp. I graze my hands over her nipples and then pinch them.

She closes her eyes and exhales. I do not want to cache her into memory but to allow everything about this to arouse me physically, chemically. My fingers slide down her stomach. It is flat and taunt, but what matters now is getting her pants off.

She kisses me as I tug at her pants and underwear. I want to make sure to get both at the same time. With my hands pulling on the elastic, she lifts her buttocks up. I slide her pants down to her ankles, pressing my face into her torso as I do. Then she draws her legs up and peels her pants off her feet as I undo my pants. She waits as I pull them off my hips.

Her knee slides across the tip of my cock as she straddles me. I slide over so she can put her foot between me and the door. She lifts her shirt, so I see her small breasts and bony chest. "Mmmm," she hums in my ear as she takes my cock and strokes it. She bounces up and down. I watch her breasts as she moves and then checks out her taut stomach. I lift my shirt because I want to feel her stomach rubbing on mine.

She keeps hold of me and strokes. This feels so great, but I can only think of being inside her. I grab her by the buttocks and pull her closer. She doesn't fight it but keeps doing what she's doing. As soon as my cock touches her pubic hair, I tremble and climax.

She wipes her hands with my shirt. Then she repositions herself, so she is sitting on my lap with her back against the door. I can tell she is going to say something, but then she leans into me and gives me a stripper kiss- exaggerated, passionless- on my cheek.

"You would not make a good veterinarian." These are my last words to her.

The passenger window across from us shatters. The door we are against opens, and we fall to the ground. Someone kicks me in the head. I see black boots and her breasts in the white light as she scrambles to get off me. Now someone pulls me out of the car and knees me in the stomach. I'm reaching for my jeans around my knees.

"Stand him up," her boyfriend says. "I knew she'd be here." His fat friend lugs on me as I struggle to get to my feet. They punch my face as I register the church doors and the spider webs on the light fixture above it. The girl scrambles out of my car, clutching her clothes.

It is not Jesse, but Jesus kicking me. Light glows behind him, and I can see his face so clearly. God's son has returned to earth to kick my teeth in. It sounds unbelievable, but He is disappointed and angry.

Then everything is bathed in blue and red lights, and a siren bleats and dies. I am dropped onto the ground.

A latex glove darts over my face. "He ain't hurt."

Then someone else, another cop. "Put your clothes on. Christ, you're my daughter's age."

23

I rub at the dried blood on my forehead. It feels like a permanent feature. Otherwise, I try not to move because every part of me is sore. Not that there is far to go in this jail cell. They asked me if I understood my charges. I answered yes because I'm not allowed to know what is really going on. I have figured that much out. My memory of what happened is unclear. Parts of last night are scattered like the wreckage of an airplane on a snowy mountainside. It's enough to know I am in jail, and I was the one attacked. The cops tried to scare me by talking about charging me with statutory rape, but the girl had just turned eighteen. Well, I sure couldn't fuck an eighteen-year-old when I was eighteen.

As for Jesus, His attack is my victory. It shows me I hurt Him where it counts.

I have been holding a bloody towel to my mouth and rinse it out in the stainless-steel sink that is part of the toilet. The water and blood I wring out pings against the basin.

"Thanks for taking me to a hospital," I snarl at a cop walking by.

"No problem," the cop mouths, not even looking at me.

"Let's get Jesus down here and clear this situation up." I punch the large window of the processing cell that looks out at officers standing around a circular counter in the middle of the room. The smell of this well-lit cell reminds me of a hospital. Piss and cleaner. I have my own stench of sweat, sex, and alcohol. In my reflection in the window, my face is bloated and discolored. I grin through the pain because of the pain. I fucked your girlfriend.

24

Rain drops through the passenger window and mixes with the shattered glass on the seat and floor as I drive. Her bra has fallen off the dashboard and is lying on the floor. The car is like me. It must stay what it is.

I park in front of Larry's office. The prefab building used to be the office of a small used car lot. The reception area has a large pane window the salesman used to watch people meander through the cars.

"Go on in, Mikey," Lisa, the secretary says as a greeting. Even when I had an appointment, she made me wait. Now I can go on in. The floor makes a hollow sound as I trudge into his office.

"Hi, Mikey," he says. "Sit down."

"I've been here a hundred times. I know to sit down."

Larry lights a cigarette, then shoves the ashtray toward me. I push it, and its smell back at him. "You quit?" I shake my head and shrug but do not answer. "Well?" he asks.

Then he says, "Mikey, I've been an agent for fifteen years. I've had you for two years now. Your show last week was the first time one of my performers didn't show up."

His window looks onto a row of backyards. A subdivision that went up when this was the outskirts of White Bear Lake. Sets of patio furniture, swing sets, plastic pools. Would I learn anything about humans if I were to explore these yards? The answer is no. Even the private play areas are staged these days.

"But that's okay. It is more than okay, Mikey." I want to take that cigarette out of his mouth and snub it on his battered metal desk. Just to let him know, I know he is doing something to get me. Otherwise, why bring it up if it's okay? He knows why I missed the show. He is the one that came and bailed me out. "It's turning out to be a great publicity stunt. Most of the Wisconsin papers ran the story, and The Tribune covered everything down to pictures of the church parking lot."

"I got over a dozen phone calls of interest about 'The Animal.' I booked a couple of them but want to see what happens before committing to too much. Entertainment Today called for some information and footage of you. Your sex scandal might go national."

He shifts in his chair and blushes to say such a thing.

"I read the articles," I lie without knowing why. I itch my face while avoiding bruised areas.

Larry stands up and walks around his desk. He now flails his arms around as he talks, and it makes me nervous. "Do you know how many viewers Entertainment Today has? You'll get the reputation that you're wild and uncontrollable. That used to mean the end of your career, but every club I deal with will want you. Heck, they already do."

He sits back down and flicks his ash onto the gray-smeared bottom of the ashtray. He is embarrassed for me and embarrassed to be my agent. I know this because he goes to church every Sunday with his wife. He always made a point to greet Mikey and Karen before service. But Larry is as professional as he is naïve.

When I stand up to leave, he stands up as well. He taps his desk several times. "The bookers are asking for a guarantee you will show up to perform, so no more publicity stunts that involve you getting thrown in jail."

His breath stinks. I tell him it smells like cigarettes and fecal matter.

25

The sun reflecting off the wet concrete and the constant difference in the speed of the other cars overwhelm me. I oversteer and break too early or too late in a panic. The hiss of wet tires pings a bone in my inner ear. Despite all this interference, the numbers Larry gave me on how successful I will be pop like dandelions on the lawn of my consciousness.

He asked me what I thought of my impending success. I told him it sounded like the right time to hire a bigger agent. He laughed because he is used to dealing with good old Mikey and underestimates me. If I gave a shit, I would get a better agent. But any success will not last, anyway. Soon my job will be in a zoo.

Maybe I cannot drive because the reflection in my rearview mirror keeps attracting my attention. My cold, hopeless eyes caged between my greasy hair and beard look back at me.

Janet lets me in without either of us saying anything. Then she sits down on the arm of one of her chairs. I roam through her apartment that is the attic of a house. The ceiling is high in the middle and slopes steeply to the walls. Her décor reminds me of every bar I've ever been to.

"Hi," I say.

"Rough weekend?" she asks, not sounding angry. She wants to let me know that she knows.

"I missed my show." She watches me go around her apartment and around her in circles. "This girl I saved from getting beat up told the police tricked me." My pants are around my ankles, and she says I started the fight.

"Oh." She slides off the armrest and into the chair. The chair's seat is deep, and she rests her arms like Captain Kirk, waiting for Sulu to plot a course to a different quadrant.

She will keep seeing me. I know enough that if she wasn't, she wouldn't have answered the door. She is actually sticking to her word and keeping things fun.

Still, I am ready for the lecture Alaine will give. "I don't want to catch no diseases from you," Janet says.

I look at her. "Nothing happened as far as penetration."

"Good. Because I really don't care. I don't, but I didn't think you were that kind of guy."

This is Wednesday. Her day off this week. So she hasn't done anything with her hair or put makeup on. Freckles paint the bridge of her nose, and her naked eyes do not stand out on her tanned face. But I am drawn to the darkness and tiredness of her eyes.

She gets up and moves toward me, but I go to the window of her door. Something in me prays that she does not look like that when I turn around. "You don't have any makeup on today."

"Haven't showered either. I'm just lying around in my own funk."

This vaguely dirty innuendo brings me to the couch. She kneels on the seat cushion next to me and puts her hand on my leg. I inhale her smell of coffee and stale smoke, but she looks so pliant I can't bear it.

"You are a lot of fun," she says. She leans close, and together we drive her vulnerability away. Her V-neck T-shirt falls forward, and I ogle her tits. I kiss her and immediately work her shirt up. She rubs my cock through my jeans. When she gets the desired effect, she draws herself up on me. "The last thing I want is any sort of commitment here. But I am looking for a little bit more than just sex," she says.

"No, you're not."

26

I drive to downtown Minneapolis. It's a little after ten, and most of the bars I wander in to have a dozen or a few dozen people in them, and most are men. I have at least one drink at each one and watch the few women out worth watching, hoping for the tragedy that just happened to me to happen again.

It won't, but this is better than going to my apartment. I couldn't stay at Janet's and make my lair inside an unfamiliar apartment and an unfamiliar woman. She might get that vulnerable look again. The thought of it makes me take two hundred dollars out of an ATM and go to a strip club.

A guy in a suit and tie takes my admission, and I find a table. A girl saunters along the edge of the stage, so I watch her instead of making eye contact with the waitress taking my order. The dancer wears a short mini-skirt and a white blouse that she awkwardly stops and unbuttons. She has bleach blonde hair, and her dancing consists of teasing her skirt down and leaning forward while pressing her breasts together with her hands. Before she is down to her G-string, I put a couple of dollars on her garter. She gives me what is supposed to be a seductive smile, puts her hands behind my head, pulls my face into her chest, and wiggles. I've worked strip clubs and have seen the girls do that and never thought it was sexy, but it makes me excitedly comforted to have her soft skin on my forehead and smell the perfume she dabbed there. For those few moments, the smoothness of her breasts against my face makes me feel human again. It's a desperate way to feel.

Upstairs, they have women get oiled up and wrestle. One of the girls seductively asks me if I would like to oil her up for twenty dollars. I rub her smooth, cool skin where her swimsuit doesn't cover. Then she smiles and thanks me. When she goes to wrestle the other girl in the ring, I go back downstairs.

Now on stage is a thirtyish woman with a huge chest. She seems popular with the other guys, but she has cellulite on her legs. It makes me see her as a mother of three kids, and I try to imagine what she does during the day until she comes into work.

A young woman I can only describe as cute asks me if I want a personal dance. She has her hair in pigtails and is wearing a tight, brief version of a cheerleader uniform. I stick a twenty on her G-string, doing it fast instead of slowly dragging my finger on her skin as a guy should. Then she dances, playing at taking her top off. She looks into my eyes, and I have to look away to check out her small chest and wide hips.

She wants to captivate me with her sexiness. To give me my money's worth, I think, but then realize she is doing it as a challenge. She wants to see in my eyes how much I want her before she takes my money and walks away. I take my beer bottle from where it is sitting between my legs on the bar stool and put it to my lips. It's empty but a way to push her away.

Afterward, she puts her clothes back on. She tells me she is a college student when I ask her if she is.

"Do you come in here a lot?" she asks.

"From now on," I say.

"Thank you," she says, touching my back with tenderness. It feels genuine, but something about this place makes me feel like I am being watched or filmed. I look around to spot the person watching me.

It's then I see Dave standing at a table with three other guys. Dave is leaning over the table like he is getting ready for a prostate exam. His friends are dressed like him with loud dress shirts, jeans, and dress shoes.

I take a drink of my empty beer as if what I will swallow will calm me down. My heart pounds. He is the one assigned to spy on me tonight.

After Dave buys two beers, he saddles up to me. "Hey, are you fucking nuts, man? I was going to call you. What the hell happened in Wisconsin?"

"Hey," I say, now cold to have come here and cold to these women, so conveniently naked.

He sits down on the barstool next to me. I turn to the girl on stage crouching down, picking up her dollar bills. "That girl you told me about, she doesn't work here, does she? Cause I don't want to be putting my face in the titties of your woman."

"No, I just came from her place in Saint Cloud."

"Yeah," he says. "Me and my friends were working on a couple of honeys earlier at Kieran's. All they wanted was us to buy them their drinks. It was dumb, but we couldn't give up until they took away our chance and went home. Why don't you come join us?"

"Did you know I was going to be here?"

"Are you drunk, Mikey? How would I know that?"

"Yeah. But I'm taking off." Saying the words makes me feel the opposite. Strip clubs are the only honest places in the twin cities. Money allows men to think of women sexually. When in history did love get invented so that man had to think beyond propagating the species?

The dancers have to do only one thing to be valued. Make men horny. Such an urge makes people weaker, but the men use the money to have control. The bigger the tip, the more dominance they establish. The dancers are obligated to give attention. They want to give it because money is survival. It's simple, direct. Close to nature. "I'm surprised that you're here with your friends. You dilute your mating by socializing."

"Mikey, this isn't 'mating' in any sense of the word. This is looking titties for kicks."

"That's right." Why couldn't I see that? "Because mating isn't fun."

"Come again? Last time I tried it–"

"Ask a male spider who gets eaten by his mate just because she's wider."

"I don't understand, Mikey,"

"It's a nursery rhyme." I take a pull of my beer. "Relax. Like you, I'm just messing around."

"Working on your new act."

"Under it, Davey. Yeah, going off the deep end is a full-time job."

Dave looks over to his friends as they yell for him to come back. "Tell me what is going on. I don't see how you can throw all your material out and start over. I couldn't."

"Yeah, that's why I should take off. I got to finish throwing the baby out with the bathwater. This is a waste of my time." Dave has done some terrible things when it comes to women. Now I have matched him and even beat him, and it's good to command the destruction of my own life. Like me, Dave can't change the direction he is taking but likes the feel of his foot on the throttle. It's why he comes here a lot.

When I don't say anything else or get up to leave, Dave says, "Yeah, I don't know why I came here. After a while, the whole thing seems sad."

Dave tells me to come down to Humphrey's tomorrow to see him, and then he goes back to his friends. They clamor for him to drink as he approaches their table and lines up two shots. Dave isn't destructing. Why am I thinking he is like me? He has all those friends and no shortage of women that will fuck him with no strings attached. No wonder this place is sad to him. It's for losers like me who can't get female contact any other way.

Another young woman asks if she can dance for me. I've had my fill of this place, but she has full lips and a petite body. Her toned flesh is the opposite of Janet's fleshy curves. I nod my head and hold out a twenty for her to take. She hooks her finger on the strap to her G-string, and I slide the money underneath. Her skin is silky and cool.

She strips her top off while giving me sexy eyes. I don't return her gaze. Her tits, perky with erect nipples in the cool, smoky air, are what I paid the money to see, but I study the space between them and her throat. Her nakedness leaves me vulnerable.

Her intelligent hazel eyes and her sly, warm smile, even her small ears with multiple piercings, contain happiness, but never for me.

When she finishes, I want to tuck another ten into her clothing to feel her inviting skin, but don't. She puts her top back on, standing next to me. I get up and walk out. It's closing time, and I don't want to see Dave on my way out.

27

Knocking wakes me up. It takes me a moment to adjust to the afternoon light and get off the floor. It turns to fist-pounding just before I see Dan and Alaine through the peephole.

"Thanks, Mike," Dan says when I let them in. Alaine whispers something to him.

"Dan. How's the computer business?" I put my hand to my chin in extreme interest to be glib, but I can't even focus my eyes on them or comprehend that they are here, together, on a Saturday afternoon. They sit on the couch when I point to it. When my eyes finally focus, I see Alaine is sitting close to him. They are here to blame me. It makes me pace behind them.

She has turned to look at me, but Dan touches the coffee table with his fingertips. "Michael, we are concerned about you."

I escape to the kitchen and open the refrigerator. There is nothing in it other than beer, so I get one out. Dan is speaking loudly. He wants this over with, and he is not the only one. Alaine being here, though, has my nerves. "Alaine was very upset when she read what you did in the paper."

"Tell her not to read the paper then."

"This is not a joke, Buddy."

"Stop it, Mike," Alaine says. "I am worried about you. You don't do that kind of stuff."

I stomp back into the living room to speak. "You were so worried about the weekend that you rushed over here first thing a week later. Jesus died, got buried, and was headed home in the time you took to show up."

"What does that mean?" She gives a puzzled look to Dan for a moment. "I can't figure out why you are mad at me, Mikey. But we are supposed to be friends."

"Friends? Friends? A friend doesn't bring a bodyguard when she visits." I point at Dan.

"We are both here to help." Dan stands up. I still tower over him but step onto the coffee table.

"You think Mikey has lost his mind. Acting weird," I tell them. "This is an improvement."

"Get down from there," Alaine says, but then turns away and mutters, "Having sex with a teenager in a church parking lot is not a step up."

"And we are not friends anymore. Don't cry about it, Dan. Alaine. It's not you. It's me not wanting you around. I got rid of all my friends."

"Why?" she asks, not looking at me.

"I just did."

She spins around. "God."

"Don't talk to me about your God. That deadbeat dad who punished his son for his own sins. Your spiteful, angry God."

Alaine stands up, but I am still far above her on the coffee table. "What Karen did was terrible," she says. "But you need to let it go. She was—"

"Shut up." I fall off the coffee table and onto the entertainment center, knocking knick-knacks off it. Out of reflex, I catch a few. "Shut up."

They rush toward me. Even though I am Dan's least favorite person, it's human nature to rush to help someone when they are in danger. They grab me and help me regain my balance.

"Mikey, your phone calls these last few weeks have been strained. You'd talk a mile a minute and then get stone silent."

Mikey's little mementos from the entertainment center fall from my hand to the floor. "Your job has turned your brain to mush. You need to get beyond your daily thoughts and worries."

"You were lonely on the road. I didn't know what to do to help you."

"I have friends in every city. They are fun and friendly and very witty."

"But my Mikey would never be so desperate as to do what you did last weekend."

Dan has snuck up behind Alaine and put his arm in front of her. "We want you to talk to someone that can prescribe some medication or something. You look terrible."

"Let's talk about love, Dan. Your lover should be your best friend, don't ya think? Me either. Because it's not possible. A relationship is the most dangerous thing to have. A lover is too much like an enemy. Because they will hurt you."

"I knew it had to do with Karen," Alaine says.

"But you guys are right." I sit down on the couch. Perhaps they will leave if I calmly explain it all to them. "All my thoughts were drowning me." These words do not sound like the truth. It leaves out Alaine's role. "You were drowning me. Why would you do that?" I stand up, now, angry. "Don't drown me."

Then I smile. "I found a secret way to keep alive." I turn and walk away like a predatory cat. A lion does not worry. He saunters around and is not distracted by what cannot benefit or threaten him. A lion walks out the door.

Halfway down the street, I glance to make sure they are not following me. But it's not important if they are. Everything else takes my attention, and that is good. Cars go by. A breeze rustles the leaves in the small trees planted on the terrace. The street signs wobble after I swat them. The blue sky and the warm sun on my face contain every answer.

28

The great thing about Saint Paul is that it is filled with unimportant things. American cars missing hubcaps and sooty trees filled my senses. Alaine and Dan do not enter my mind until I come back to my apartment. It makes me chuckle how I ignored Alaine completely and managed politeness to Dan. I should apologize to him just to crush Alaine.

I dance and sing around my apartment, taking swigs of my warm, flat beer. "She's hurt. She's mad." To me, that's too funny. Once the beer is gone, I plop down on the couch and rest the empty can on my stomach. It rises and falls with my big breaths.

Then I am walking the business district where people in suits are hurrying about. Like a dog wearing a sweater, I have put on a suit as well. But people smile at me. A few say hi. That has never happened before. The wind blows my open suit and whips my tie in an enjoyable way. I smooth my hair with my hand and say hi back to those that say hi to me.

The wide, clean sidewalks lead me past the manicured entrances of the buildings. Small trees protected by intricate cast-iron grates have cherry blossoms. Overhead, glass skywalks glimmer like balconies at a giant theater. The buildings are tall and shiny or solid and comforting.

I cross the light at Jackson and Sixth. Jesse is waiting in a car, the greasy boyfriend who beat me up. He scratches at a scraggy beard and revs the engine until I am in front of him. Then he presses down on the gas pedal. His whole body twists with effort as the car lunges for me. I run like hell and somehow jump out of the way, and he hits another car. It's my car, The Beast. I wonder who is driving it.

It's Mikey in his car, trapped behind the mangled door. Completely an animal now, I'm able to leave Mikey out of this. To make sure Jesse leaves him alone, I run down the middle of the street. My legs feel like they are going to fly out from under me. I keep losing my footing as if running on snow. Jesse is closing in. If I can get to Alaine's apartment, I will be safe. It is miles away but the only place for safety.

The battered car weaves through traffic to get to me. He's not alone. The car is filled with people, all cheering him on. I am heading toward the Mississippi River. Hoping he has turned off, I glance back to see only Karen sitting next to Jesse.

I am in an all-out sprint when I come to a cliff. There's nothing I can do to stop and fall into the canyon the river has carved out.

Falling face forward, I somehow grab onto a flagpole. No, it's a small tree growing out of the rock.

Someone falls past me. It looks like that girl, my attacker's girl. She falls and falls. At the bottom of the canyon is the church where we had sex. I walk up to it. It towers over me, taller than that night. The girl is still falling. She is a speck in the sky until she hits the church and is punctured by the spire. It's pointed like a lance. I am back hanging on the tree with a top view of the girl sprawled on top of the church. She had to go first, but soon I will fall. The same will happen to me.

I sit up on the couch and pound the armrest.

"Are you trying to intimidate me, God?" I yell. "Should I repent because of a dream? Dogs dream. Don't tell me You are trying to protect the innocent. That girl was already corrupted.

"And You don't protect the innocent, anyway. Do You?"

The clock on the VCR says 8:00. Warm sunlight shines through the patio door. How long have I slept?

It's Sunday. Goddamn, Sunday morning. I have on the clothes I wore to meet with Larry.

I stumble outside to the parking lot. My keys are in my hand.

29

I sit in The Beast in front of the church. The small, white-sided building is just off the freeway but set among upper-middle-class homes. It almost looks like a house except for the stained-glass windows and the double wooden doors open to let parishioners in.

Mikey would walk into this church with his hand in Karen's. He wore slacks and a button-down shirt, feeling the tightness of his dress shoes. This was the church Karen's parents attended before they moved out to Vadnais Heights and the one Karen wanted to get married in. Larry and his wife greeted them before heading in, and sometimes her parents drove in and sat in the same pew

Mikey had always believed in God and went to church every Sunday with his grandma. In college, he found comfort and courage in the way Reverend's sermon seemed to always be speaking to him. But it wasn't until he went with Karen that he believed God provided happiness on earth.

Even Mikey eventually found the folly in that.

Men in Khaki's and tennis shoes herd their wives and children up the steps. A few people are in shorts, but most are wearing respectable outfits—so many daughters in bright dresses.

The people walking into the church shine. Some are poor. Some are humble. Some are not. These people stand next to their loved ones and before their God. The priest will tell them they are blessed, and they will look at their spouses and kids and parents and smile. They are chosen, but not by merit.

I get out of the car. "If You think I came to repent, You're crazy." I have the tire iron from the trunk in my hand and fling it with all the exertion I can muster into one of the stained-glass windows.

The glass shatters, the shards rain down to tell me that was wrong to do.

"Don't tell me to go to Hell." The windows don't get to have the last word.

Then I take off in the car, hitting the first left and flying down the streets until I am back on 494.

30

My dressing rooms used to be the men's toilet. Finally, my dressing room has no urinals. Ha. Ha. The spacious room has paneled walls and a leather couch. It even has a TV and a phone. It has a mini refrigerator to keep my beer cold.

November in Minnesota, and I am home after some big gigs on the road. Fucking yawn. I was supposed to call Janet hours ago, and now it will be busy at the bar. This better be her answering the phone. "Whistle Stop Station."

"It's me."

"Hi, honey," Janet says, her voice mingled with the noise of the bar behind her, around her, and in front of her. "We're packed. You should see the customers glare at me because I am on the phone."

"They want me to do a meet and greet after the show," I tell her. "They think they can work me like a dog just because they gave me a big dressing room."

"I know you're stressed out, hon. I'm sorry as hell for you. Are you coming over afterward?"

"Well, how late are you going to be? I don't want to wait for hours watching you clean up."

"I'm so ready for some sexy time. I could close up early."

That's her way of telling me she didn't sleep with anyone else during my absence. "The sooner you get off, the sooner you'll get off." The alarm clock on the end table tells me it's show time. "All right, gotta go." I hang up the phone and check myself in the big, lighted mirror. My hair is an Afro gone bad. I have a whole can of hairspray in it. My beard hangs off my chin, mangled with more hair spray. I lift it to my nose. God, it stinks.

My costume is bib overalls and a ragged flannel shirt. I pick up a leather studded collar with a three-foot metal chain on it and clasp it around my neck. Then I stuff gauze in my mouth and apply the enamel that makes my teeth appear yellow and decayed. This is the outfit Larry had made for me by someone he knows.

The announcer speaks with the microphone too close to his mouth. "I'm afraid everyone here is in danger. Please remain calm, but a wild animal" –the crowd cheers– "as escaped from a nearby zoo. It is loose somewhere in this club and extremely unpredictable." Colored lights flash on the stage and strobe around the audience. Music booms out the sound system. "Grrrawwl." I am still coming up a dark hallway that leads to the stage.

The set is supposed to be the interior of a cave representing my home. It has a bed of straw and various props for me to destroy. Garland and lights are strung along the proscenium arch, and a large Christmas tree sits on stage right.

When I jump at the announcer, he plays along and runs from the stage, but he is pissed. While the crowd loves it, I am under strict orders to leave him alone. Some women scream. I want that announcer gone.

I bare my teeth at the crowd. Then I swing the long chain connected to the shackle around my neck and make the front row duck. With the chain spinning, I check out the crowd. As usual, there are more chicks than dicks in the audience. They like this violence even more than men do.

That should spur me on to do a great show. Mechanically, I go through my stunts- me breaking things and throwing myself into break-away furniture. I pantomime a skit where I explore a little home like Goldilocks, except I break stuff and end up with food all over me.

My act does have a few jokes, and I want to get them out of the way. Perhaps then, I can give the crowd something unplanned.

No words come out. I stomp to the kitchen table that had been set up for a fancy dinner until I "explored" it. It splinters apart when I belly flop onto it. The prop cups and plates are scatter on stage. I stand up.

Then I walk out of the cave set and grab the Christmas tree on the apron. I hold it over my head. It wants me to kick the snot out of it, so I oblige by throwing it down and kicking it to the back curtain.

I am in front of these people with no idea what to do next. There are other stunts arranged for me to do, but I do not know what they are. The lights are bright, and it is hot. This is a terrible event. My signature sign-off is the only thing left to do. "I hate you fucking people!"

The crowd shrieks with joy as I run up and down the aisles. Before running out, I beat my stomach the way Tarzan beat his chest.

31

The security door to Alaine's apartment building opens. It's not Alaine, and that should be my sign to leave. Though I just went out for a drive, this was my destination the whole time. I did not come home to see Janet or run up to Duluth for Thanksgiving but to sit here in my car.

Alaine always had a life to keep her busy when Mikey was on the road, but I can't imagine what she does. I am not here to talk to her or see if she looks any different. Fear of one thing brings me here. It's a constant fear that someone will come and freeze me in a cage of time. It may have happened already. Though my behavior changes every day, my life has been the same for the last six months. Performing, traveling, copulating leaves me empty. So while I pretend to be parked here to celebrate my victory over Alaine, I need this moment of sitting in Mikey's car and feeling something.

Just for an hour or two. Then I will be done with being human. There was so much traveling and too much of nothing to sleep. On the road, the animal was tired. Is tired. So tired that I must walk on the hot coals of my old life to release my numbness.

There were times when I wanted to be Mikey Haskell and call

Alaine. Mostly this was after being in my hotel room for a few hours. The dark and quiet room around me and the clunking of doors closing in the hallway hinted that this was when Mikey enjoyed telling Alaine about his day. It was Pavlovian.

A figure comes to stand in their kitchen window. Perhaps Dan and Alaine are happily doing the dishes together. Part of me still believes she can only be happy with me. It's clear that it's the other way around, but I don't want happiness. I want to get close enough to see it and then leave before it hurts too much.

Alaine comes out the front door and down the steps with a sweater wrapped around her. When she waits for a car to go by, I take off.

32

A second night of being home. I have remembered all the stunts tonight. All around me is the debris of my act. Instead of ending the show, I jump off the stage and run through the crowd growling at them. Women are reaching out to grab me, and the men slap me on the back. I stop in front of a good-looking woman. She is short, and I lean over and smell her hair.

Next to me, a man holds out a flask. I throw the contents of the flask at my open mouth. The crowd around me flinches to avoid getting wet, but the whole auditorium loves it. The remnants of my comedic instinct tells me to build on this reaction, but my nerves are ruined. At full speed, I run back onto the stage. The announcer's microphone in its stand grabs my attention. Mikey loved to stand in front of a microphone, and this makes me rotate around it and poke it with a finger. The tap goes over the speakers. Then I sniff into it, and the sound reverberates out the sound system like a strong wind. Finally, I grate my teeth on it, just to hear that.

I give a sideways glance at the crowd. All the people are laughing or growling. They want to be an animal like me. And maybe that is what I am doing- starting a religion. I am the second coming of

Christ. Here to lead the people back to natural lives and away from God.

As I hate myself, so shall I hate God.

They are standing and cheering me except for one woman sitting off to my right alone. Alaine. Around her, people are chanting, "Animal. Animal." I look at her again, expecting her to be someone else now.

She is sitting there staring at me. Her eyes are puffy. She mouths, "Why?"

"Son-of-a-fucking-bitch." I jump off the stage again and paw through the crowd. The people in her row twist in their seats so I can get to her. She doesn't need to be here and torture me. How dare she reject me? My hands go to hurt her- to divert myself, I pick her up and throw her over my shoulder.

She pounds on my back. "Stop. Don't," she screams. "Don't." She is a sack of fear over my shoulder. I set her down on the stage and step back into the audience.

"Look what I find," I tell the crowd. "I good hunter. I find prey."

She stands there. The crowd laughs. I get up on stage and spin around her in a savage dance. Then I glare from behind her. A white light comes up to spotlight Alaine, and it excites me that this light has found her. She looks tiny, like a child.

I lunge for her as two guys grab me and pull me off the stage and into the hallway that leads to the dressing rooms. They let go, and I fall to the floor, but the audience is cheering for the night to end like that.

The stage manager is over me. "What the fuck are you doing? She'll sue me. How fucking sadistic are you?" I do not answer, so I can hear the crowd applaud me.

Janet is waiting for me inside the dressing room, reading one of her chick-lit books. She did not see anything of what went on. I shut the door in front of the stage manager, who is still hounding me. Janet drapes herself on me like a harness.

33

Dave is knocking and calling me. I throw my blankets off and get up off the floor. It is a gray morning, and I turn on the lights even though it's almost noon. When I open the door, he is standing there—the same old Dave.

"You haven't been down to Humphrey's for a while, so I came to check on you."

"Sorry, man. I've been on the road." I back a comfortable distance from him, kicking my blankets out of the way, and lead him into the living room. Dave is a friend of someone that is no longer me. All he does is remind me of the price I have paid for my invincibility.

"Well, you've been home for a few days now. You're not pissed at me for anything, are you?"

"What?" When was the last time I saw him? At the strip club? I wonder if he would visit me if I wasn't getting so famous. "No. Things have been a little intense."

Dave sits down and adjusts a pizza box tittering off the side of the coffee table. It has been there a while because cigarettes are snubbed out in it, and I haven't smoked in months. He looks around my filthy living room and then at me. "Still sporting the Bobcat Goldthwait on steroids look," he says. "80s version, of course." I haven't had a haircut or shaved since May. Last night, I didn't bother to take a shower to get the hairspray out of my hair.

"My look is selling a lot of tickets."

"Mike. I can appreciate that. But the thing is, you act so different too. It's like you're on drugs or something."

I'm looking at my bare feet. It takes me a while to say anything. But I want Dave to hear my new philosophy. "I'm just doing what I need to survive."

"Okay," he says. "But what the hell does that mean?"

I wander into the dining room, where my rehearsal mirror is set back up. Every day I check to see how much more of me is covered in hair. My hair is piled on my head now and down to my shoulders. My beard is full and bushy. I even like how tired my eyes look. "It means the life you save may be your own. I stopped caring about what other people think."

"That's good, I guess. You gotta do what you want and let the chips fall where they may. But it's more than that. You're not acting anything like yourself."

Dave has a fresh haircut and wired-rimmed glasses. The summer lounge lizard has made his own transformation to a respected member of the faculty.

"You know, maybe I should come see your new act. I haven't seen you do the animal yet."

"I don't do the animal. I am the animal. But don't bother seeing the act. It's bad."

"Aren't you concerned about that?" Dave, the-I-gotta-be-Mikey's counselor, says.

"Shit, no. It's the gimmick making me rich and famous. Without rehearsing or coming up with new material. All I gotta do is let loose—"

He shakes his conspiratorial head at me. "This is not you, Mikey. Running around on stage and picking up strangers in bars."

"What the fuck do you know? Or are you afraid I will horn in on your sluts?"

"Don't push me away, Mike."

"I'm not one of your troubled students. Okay?" I'm losing the ability to speak. Give me summer, Dave. Let's talk about getting drunk and going to strip bars.

"I'm not letting this drop. Look at how you are living. Look at yourself."

"Fuck you. You look at yourself." He talks to me and tries to get me to respond, but I sit staring until he gets up and leaves. For a long time, I study the two cigarette butts snubbed out in the pizza box. The grease spots soaked into the box and the crusted cheese are a set for a play in a pizza box amphitheater—the two cigarette actors doing the final scene in Romeo and Juliet.

* * *

Before I tire of the play, there is a knock on the door.

It is a pair of officers from The Hennepin County Sheriff's Department, and they stand like a wall in front of my door. "Mr. Michael James Haskell?"

"Yes."

The one doing the talking introduces himself as Officer Owens. He is tall but shorter than me and has a big, raw, clean face. The other one is shorter with a closely clipped mustache. "May we come in?" Owens asks. My denial doesn't seem to affect them at all.

"Okay. We just need to hand you this." Mustache hands me several sheets stapled together and folded over. "This is a Harassment Order prohibiting you from any contact with Alaine Varnes."

"What? Who sent you, you lackeys, you minions?"

"Pipe down," raw face says.

"The Harassment Order is a temporary restraining order until your hearing on December 18th. If you do not attend the hearing, the judge may grant this order by publication, and it will go into effect. You may not contact Ms. Varnes by phone or any other agent."

"Why not?"

"Come on, Mr. Haskell," Owens says. "You know better than we do."

"No. No, I don't." I step closer to them, wanting to crush them for embarrassing me. "Would you guys like to come in for coffee and discuss this?"

Owen widens his stance and points open palms at me. "Sir, the Order to Show Cause and Temporary Restraining Order states you allegedly attacked her during your performance at The Ritz Theater, 345 13th Avenue, and was stopped by security before you did great bodily harm."

"Do you get it now?" Thin Face utters,

"No. But I don't have any coffee." I take the paper from them and shut the door. "Bitch. Bitch." How could she do this? Wasn't I in enough trouble with the cops? I can see her true colors finally. She is straightforward, trying to pay me back. Something she started.

34

Janet moans and bucks on top of me. Her swaying tits invite me to touch them, but I'm angry from her foreplay where she was drawing things out by wanting a backrub first. I only kept at it because we're in a strange dressing room in a new city, and it excited me to hear people walking by in the hall.

She has become difficult. Sometimes she wants me to not be able to keep my hands off her. Other times, she gets hurt if we don't talk first.

She stops, flops onto me, and whispers, "Go ahead and come if you want." She says this a lot, but if I do too soon, then she complains I don't care about her. I guide her over and get on top. Her face is against my chest, and my arms are uncomfortably holding me up. The sensation is more intense, but I'm getting out of breath and will not climax this way.

We are both ready to stop, but my lack of an orgasm will make her feel ugly. This puts pressure on me. Sex with Janet has become like breaking into a safe. I have to align everything right at the right moment and get her door open with no alarms going off.

She gets on all fours, and I slide into a new sensation, put the palm of my hand on her tailbone. Her ass jiggles as I thud into it with my thighs, but I can't finish until footsteps approach and someone tries the locked door handle. This is what excites me enough.

* * *

The floor gets too cold just as I am about to fall asleep. When I open my eyes, Janet is putting her underwear on. She pulls the elastic waistband up to the roundness of her belly. Then she leans over and drapes her bra over her breasts before reaching to do the hooks. As I predict, she puts her sweater on next because she wants to cover her stomach as soon as possible before stepping into her pants. The peach of her underwear disappears as she buttons and zips her jeans.

She crosses her arms and looks at the wall above my head. "Mikey, what are we supposed to be doing here?"

At first, I want to ask her if she is here in my dressing room in Seattle, where I paid her airfare. But even as I am, I know what she is really asking. Women do not put a bra on to have things to discuss. "Having fun. Having our day in the sun."

"Having fun."

"That's what you said you wanted."

"You were exactly what I wanted. Big, funny, crazy. But that was July, and this is December."

What does the kind of precipitation have to do with anything? "Are we having this conversation because I wouldn't go to that family get-together with you?"

"It was Thanksgiving. But we are having this conversation because I thought you invited me here for a romantic weekend. But you want to do me here in the dressing room just to say you did. Then afterward, you don't say a word. I care about you, Mikey. But all I am is somebody to have sex with."

"No shit, Janet." I'm so exhausted. "That is what you were looking for. So what are you saying? Are we breaking up?"

"I think so. Yes."

"You want to break up now? After I flew you out here?"

She comes over to stand above me. "You've grown so cold."

The retort in my head is I've been cold right from the start.

"This whole trip, I could have been anyone for all you cared."

"What does that mean? Could a woman explain what they mean for once?"

She cries without hiding how it contorts her face. "I've been blindly in love before and don't want to be fucked over by empty promises again. This isn't any better, though. You don't even want my love."

"That doesn't mean a fucking thing. It's just something for you to say." She planned on saying it all along. "Who told you to say that?"

"This isn't a joke." She looks at me for one single moment more. "I can't let you put me through this."

"Fine," I say. "I don't need you to start my own religion." I hadn't thought of it before, but she could have been my Eve. Carnal, horny Eve for my paradise. She ate the fruit of emotions and experienced the pain of love for her transgression. As God said, you cannot be weak and remain in paradise.

She slips her shoes on as I get up and put the bib overalls from my costume on. "See? You are always making comments like that. Doing your animal act on stage is one thing, but to insist on doing it all the time is just sick."

She has the keys to the rental car and a key to the hotel room, so when she walks out, I sit back down. No matter what I do, I am rejected. I expect anger to hit me like a wave, but it doesn't. It makes me laugh at how it doesn't get to me. In the mirror, the bright lights contrast my dark body hair. Without a shirt on, I see how my facial hair is not a beard but a continuation of my coat from my chest, up to my neck, and to my face.

35

MIKEY'S PAST

Mikey studied Karen's chewed fingernails as she held her notebook down to write. He liked sitting on the first floor of the library because they took a table by a window, and he could watch the weather and the empty courtyard getting light and dark as clouds marched in their giant parade.

As she printed, she drew a long strand of her chestnut hair and twirled it. This was one of her habits when she was tired, and Mike had been waiting for it. He reached across and caressed her writing arm.

With her head still bent to the textbook, Karen looked at him. 'I've got to study, Michael."

"Yeah, me, too." His book was opened to a random page. He picked it up and turned it, so he was looking at it upside down. She gave a slow shake of her head but smiled. "Okay. You keep on studying that, and I'll just watch you."

"I can't study with you looking at me. If you want to go do something, you can. You're bored."

"We're studying." There was nothing he needed to do at the

moment to pass his classes. Not that he cared anymore if he passed them or not. Stand-up was what he was going to do. He had ten paid gigs under his belt already.

"You're not. If you want to go find Alaine-"

"I want to marry you."

"I know that. And I want to marry you. I wish we were done with school."

"No. Will you marry me?

"I was going to ask you tonight. I have a ring back at my apartment." He slid his chair out and stood up. "I don't want to make a scene, but this is all I can think about."

"If this is a ploy to get me to stop studying, Michael James," she whispered. She called him Michael James because it was dramatic, and she was young. "It worked."

She threw herself at him while wrapping her arms around his neck. He scooped her up, and then spun around until too many people were watching them.

36

Alaine and Janet think they can break me. But they can't get to me. None of them can. I gave them enough warning of what they are dealing with. Like they couldn't tell by looking at me, I am invincible. It's time to fight back.

"Larry. Larry–" I am calling him back about doing a night at Whistle Stop Station before I go do some big clubs out in Los Angeles. He is talking about favors and how the owner is an old friend.

"Larry, will you shut up? I'll do it." I look out my window to the alley below. There is a thin layer of snow over the garbage bags.

"For the deal he's suggesting? He can only give you a cut from the door, but this could bring in large numbers. Local comic comes home after making it big, and The Animal comes back to where he was born. He's going to raise the cover."

"Yes." I fog the window with my breath.

"You'll do it? I owe you one," Larry tells me.

"All you have to do is have him fire one of his bartenders. Janet Anderson. I will do it for free if he gets rid of her."

"Are you serious, Mikey? I can't ask him that."

He lets me go around and make a fool of myself and get into trouble, but he won't ask that? "You can, and you will."

"Come on, Mikey. Whatever your problem with her was, you're bigger than that. Why do it?"

"Life is a merry-go-round, Lar. Sometimes people get pushed off." I listen to him breathe on the other end and then hang up.

Now and next. I kick through my clothes on the floor, looking for my car keys. The pizza boxes and paper plates from my coffee table scatter to the floor as I unbury them. I jingle the keys and laugh. What I will do is not much, but it will work, and it will be enough for now.

Out in the parking lot, the wind carries hard snow with it. It blows through the tattered plastic covering the broken window of my car as I crank it over and get it started.

The car slides and spins sideways on the snow. I have been flying and taking taxis for so long, driving the car is foreign to me. So is the city, this familiar route.

The mid-priced vehicles of Alaine's neighborhood have driveways, and Alaine's apartment complex has a basement garage. Alaine will see The Beast parked across from her entrance.

Under her window, she will believe I am nearby, maybe even crouched down in the car, lurking and breaking the court order. She will be scared. The court order proves I terrify her, and she has always been afraid of being attacked. It's why she doesn't like being alone.

The door to The Beast creaks open. I fling the keys under the front seat so that I can be rid of this car. Then I slam the door and hope Alaine hears it.

She can't because she is still at work. Because of her, everything of Mikey is gone, so let her dispose of his car. The last thing of him.

I take large, hard steps. The distance home only gives me more time to celebrate my victory. Being in control makes me high.

Mostly, I am alone on the sidewalk. People drive everywhere these days, but I will know the freedom of the scented trail. As I get closer to a commercial area, the light traffic of people steps out of my way. One guy slides around me with great caution, even though he has enough room. Then a rougher guy gives me a wide berth. As people slink by, I dwarf them like they are children.

A woman in a soft, furry parka comes out of an apartment building and walks slowly on the sidewalk. I measure her, too. She is ten feet away, but I figure she only comes to my rib cage.

I am a god walking among humans, but all animal. My feet pound on the sidewalk as the bracing air hit my face. The woman in the parka crosses the street, and I keep pace behind her. A car could hit me, and I would not feel it. And while this woman does not glance back, I sense her fear. At the next corner, she turns to avoid me, and I walk on.

The coldness has gotten to my hands, and it is making my nose run. I wipe the snot away on my arm. What I can walk is my territory. I own it. You can't possess your dominion in a car.

My legs are tight from walking, but I keep a pace to overtake anyone walking in front of me, size them up, and determine where they are in my pecking order without having to fight.

37

It's dark and snowing by the time I reach Planned Parenthood. I walk in expecting to find a waiting room of teenage girls, but it is empty and quiet.

"One moment, please," the receptionist tells me when I ask for Dan Price. She looks at me and hesitates but picks up the phone.

He comes from an office down a hallway. I let him pull me away from the receptionist and into the waiting area.

"We never hit it off," he says in an excited whisper. "But Alaine thought a great deal of you, and you forced us into getting that restraining order. What are you doing coming into my place of work smelling bad and looking like a bum? If you come here again or near my wife, I will have you arrested."

He has his fingers wrapped as far as they will go around my bicep. I pull out the letter she wrote to me after their biggest break-up.

I know each word he reads.

Mikey,
We've become so close over the past few weeks
And I don't know what I would have done without you.

This morning, when I woke up in your arms, I felt so safe and loved.

I will be stronger now because Karen needs you more than you'll ever

know, and I feel totally guilty about last night because you should have

been with her.

Love, Alaine

Mikey found her in bed. As they talked, he ended up under the covers and holding her. When she finished crying, he kissed her on her forehead like one of his sisters. Yet, in the morning, Mikey felt guilty because he had been lonely too with Karen studying so much. That was why Alaine wrote the letter and slipped it into his car. Mikey had kept it as a keepsake, a memory of a beautiful, sad night experienced by two friends. I look at it with disgust. How could someone lie next to a woman and hold her warm, smooth skin and be a pussy about making it physical?

Now I've handed it to her boyfriend to give credence to his jealousy.

He crumples it up and sneers at me. "Ask her," I say to make it less likely that he will believe her when he confronts her. I walk out into the cold.

Justice. Justice. Justice. The word rings in my head. I pound my clenched fist on my forehead, relishing my toughness.

38

At Humphrey's, Dave is lounging with the two other comics and the waitstaff as they fold silverware into napkins. Dave will be busy as the emcee tonight, but I want to celebrate my success.

My feet are wet and cold, and I have been walking for so long that at first, I think I won't be able to speak.

"Mikey," Dave calls out. "You look like hell."

"It's a long walk back from there." I take off my gloves but leave my jacket on to get warmed up. Then I sit in a booth adjacent to where everyone is seated. I took a bus from Saint Paul over to Minneapolis, but I've walked that distance in wandering since then.

"In the middle of winter?" he asks me. From where I have chosen to sit, conversation will be impossible.

"I stopped and visited friends." I nod to the other comedians; one of them is also a frequent guest on The Jay and Tim radio show.

Their conversation goes on, but I miss most of what is said. It's like watching a documentary of Mikey's life with the sound turned down. Someone shuts the door to the kitchen, and snippets of conversation waft toward me. "If I had my own sitcom...On these shows, the husband is always fat with a hot wife...Richer than

Prince...ever been to his nightclub...not since Chuckles closed down... I was riffing with my two buddies last night...Yeah, we were a little stoned...If you're funnier, why does he have his own show."

Dave transfers his drink, cigarettes, and himself over to my booth. Looking at him, I realize he wouldn't understand my victory. I can at least talk to him, though. "How's tonight looking?" I ask—an automatic question.

"Okay. With Donny headlining, we should be packed. Something this place never is anymore."

One of the hostesses comes to the backroom in a fur coat. Her cheeks are red as she gives Dave a friendly but lingering kiss. She is older than the waitresses folding silverware, but her good looks have a permanence to them. Instead of make-up and push-up bras, she is simply who she is. Alaine will be like that when she gets older.

The hostess walks away. Dave is distracted from our conversation by watching her, so I ask him the question on my mind. "Lions eat their young. Does God hate them for it?"

"What?" He laughs. "That is fucked up."

"Do you realize that we are mostly animals? There is a 98% similarity between apes DNA and human DNA."

"Yeah, I've heard that. Is this part of your new act?" He raises an eyebrow.

"It's my epiphany, not an act. We are animals wearing these costumes of humanness."

"Animalism? We're more than animals. But I'm all for being more natural. Getting rid of our hang-ups and made-up rules."

"No." There is no word for what I am. "You can become an actual animal if you let it come to the surface and shed everything away."

"What everything?"

My hands tremble. "All of it. People fall in love and make promises we are not capable of carrying out. For richer, for poorer. For better or worse. Four times a week until you make me pregnant.

Concern for others gets pushed aside as soon as it's inconvenient, anyway. Why deal with it?

"You don't know what I am talking about, do you?"

"I think I do."

"No, you don't."

The hostess that kissed Dave sits down at our table with a basket of french fries. "You're that comic that destroys stuff on stage, aren't you?"

"Something like that."

"It's more than an act," Dave says. "We're talking right now on how to get in touch with our carnal side."

"Right up your alley, Dave," she says.

"Hey, if it feels good, do it."

"Not even that," I say. "Joy always has a price." This woman looks like a woman from a Virginia Slims ad. Still, she evokes implicit memories of Alaine. "Joy comes from wanting something and getting it. Once you lose it, though, you know you would have been better off never getting it."

This woman slides her basket of fries as an offering to Dave and then me. "Little kids spend their days just doing things they enjoy, and they are happier than anybody. I think we should just refuse to grow up."

I answer her too loudly. "And little kids are closer to animals than we are. Did you ever notice they don't share? And if they get mad, they lash out without being sorry. We make them say it, but they aren't."

The hostess looks at me. "You have to be responsible for what you do."

"Why?"

Dave leans forward. "Because you will hurt people, and you will end up alone."

I stand up. "But I won't care. I don't care." I walk through the building and then out of it without putting on my hat and gloves.

39

"It didn't work. They impounded your car immediately," Alaine tells me over the phone.

"Why are you calling me," I say. "What are you doing?"

"Letting you know you don't frighten me." Her voice says otherwise. "So mouth breathe into the phone all you want."

I am out of breath from dragging a new mattress up the flight of stairs to my apartment. A few nights ago, I impressed a woman enough with fame to bring her home. She didn't want to stay in the living room because it was so dirty, and no one is to go into the bedroom. The new mattress needs to be placed on the floor of the dining room, so I don't have time to tell Alaine how well things are going.

"Maybe later. Is Dan there?"

"How could you ask that after what you did?"

"Oh. You sound scared," I say.

"And maybe I am. But I am still calling you. Mikey," she says. Hearing her say my name is like old times. "I let myself believe you would work things out for yourself. So I am trying to tell you what you need to hear now. Trying to terrorize me is sick. You need to get help because you are sick." She hangs up the phone.

I have arranged Mikey's practice mirror to make the dining room into a love lair. It shatters when I shove it into the wall. Alaine has made me ashamed of my victory.

40

MIKEY'S PAST

Mikey called Karen's parents. Her mother made small talk. She asked him if he was coming over for Thanksgiving or if he was going home to Duluth. Mike hesitated. Karen was bringing him home to meet her aunts and uncles. That was the plan. "Oh, here she is, Michael."

"Hello."

"Where are you?" Mikey asked.

"I decided to come home for the weekend."

Mikey did not know what to say. He didn't want to be angry, but he wanted her to explain and say she was sorry for disappearing. "I had to find out from your roommate where you were."

"Mike, I tried to call you, but you weren't home. I had a doctor's appointment and then some errands to do for my mom."

"You sound angry."

"Don't put this on me. You know I don't need your permission to go places, right? And I don't have to spend every moment of the day with you. It makes me wonder if you are ready to get married. It makes me wonder."

"No, Kare. I'm not that way. Okay?" She didn't answer, and for a few moments, nothing was said. "Are we going to be together for Thanksgiving? Your mother sounded like she didn't know I was coming."

"She does that. She asks questions she already knows the answer to." Her voice wavered. "But if you would rather visit your family without me, go right ahead. It will be a lot more exciting than coming here."

"What's the matter, Kare? Are you all right?"

For a moment, nothing. Then she sighed into the phone. "Wait. I'm going to my room." Mikey heard her climb the stairs with the cordless phone. He didn't hear her door shut, but he knew she had shut it when she picked up the handset in her bedroom and clicked off the other one. He heard the silence of her room.

"Karen."

"I had a doctor's appointment today to confirm the test I took last week."

Mikey almost waited for the punchline. One that would explain why she didn't tell him she was sick. "What did you find out?"

Her voice was distant. As if she was holding the receiver away from her mouth. "I'm pregnant."

The emotion that made it to his consciousness was anger that she had known for a while and didn't tell him. The amount of anger he thought he would never feel toward her. Because she had not told him and because she was the messenger and because she was not happy about it. But he refused to allow any emotion in his voice. "Pregnant." He stood in his kitchen. His hand trembled as it held the phone.

"I'll come over."

"Don't. I haven't told my parents yet."

"They're going to notice."

"Meet me at my apartment. My roommates are gone. I'll call you when I get there."

Mike waited three hours for her to call and drove over to her apartment. What worried Mike as he drove was that he wasn't happy about it either. There would be her parents to tell and his mom. They would have to find a priest to marry them and have a fast wedding.

He wanted to kiss her as soon as he saw her, but she opened the door, and he didn't. After a few moments, they moved into the apartment without speaking

Both sat down on the couch, and they were face to face without moving. She kissed him. They couldn't stop kissing and holding each other. It wasn't until Karen got up that they moved to her bedroom and made love.

He did not know what this meant. To be making love. But lying together in her bed afterward, he noticed she was not with him. She gave no reaction to him as he lay close to her and stroked her arm. "At least you'll graduate before the baby is born," he said. "The timing could be worse. And at least we are engaged.

"I'll find a good job, Karen, and when the baby is a little older, you can go to graduate school."

She was still not there with him.

"We could even do this without you missing school. Kids can go into daycare after six weeks. I just need to get a good enough job." Mikey wanted to tell her how good he was at taking care of his sisters.

Her voice was harsh. "That's seven years later to have another kid."

"You have four more years of school."

"It will take at least two years after that to get settled into a practice. My children are going to have brothers and sisters to play with." She stopped and held her mouth closed; her lower lip pursed.

"You don't have to be a veterinarian. Lots of people end up doing something other than what they went to school for."

"You wouldn't understand. You don't care what kind of job you get."

Mikey thought she was the one that didn't understand. He was only who he wanted to be up on the stage. But he would give it up. "Then we will do whatever it takes for you to go to graduate school."

"It has to be the University of Virginia."

An urge welled between his shoulder blades to yell at her for waiting all day to tell him about the baby. For not telling him she suspected she was pregnant when she bought the test. "Then we'll move to Virginia. I'll get a job there."

"What kind of job are you going to get? Not a good one. Remember all those jokes you make about me supporting you?"

Mike got up and struggled into his clothes. Then he sat on the edge of the bed. To leave meant the end of things being perfect and of Karen being perfect. Karen was already different. But to take the action of leaving would make the last year not have happened.

He waited for her to take stock of what she said and apologize. He needed hopeful words he could carry home on the front seat of his car. Whatever fights they had next, these words would be packed away to show his son or daughter when they were older.

"I can't ruin all I have worked for," she said, rolling over and turning to stone.

41

The people on the bus have never seen anything like me. They paid attention to where I sit down and glance back at me.

Janet tricked me. I called Whistle Stop Station to talk about my cut of the show, and she answered the phone. She was ending a laugh as she brought the receiver to her mouth. Now I need to see the damage. She should have let herself be fired. It would have been easier on her.

This time I will not keep the peace while someone does whatever she likes to me. "No more, Mr. Nice Guy," I say to the others on the bus. "That's why."

The bus ride took three hours. The last bus for the Twin Cities leaves at 12:30. That leaves me plenty of time, but I zip my jacket and put my gloves on so I can rush into the night.

The other riders stay seated until I bound off the bus. Janet will fear monsters long after tonight. Well, she used me for a free trip to Seattle. That disrespect requires retaliation. Aggression will teach her a lesson. Alaine's voice was angry, nervous when she called me. Yet, I hit myself in the head to get her words out of my mind. Because

I can only imagine her fear and can only guess what Dan said when he confronted her. It is not enough of a victory.

My ears are cold. Counting on my hairy face and long hair, I didn't bring a hat. There is no wind, but it must only be in the teens. The cold seems to make everything quiet. There are no people out or any cars going down the road. There are only ice-covered branches and mounds of snow in the darkness. The snow mutes the shapes, the colors, and the sounds of the grass, the houses, and the sidewalks. Everything is insulated and snuggled except me. People have their drapes pulled back to show off the lights on their Christmas trees through the squares of their windows. I don't see the people in the houses, but their walls reflect the flickering lights of TV sets. They may not know it, but I'm making this territory mine.

This is the right road, but I do not know how much farther to go. Janet deserves to experience the power around her and then for it to pierce her skin. Why didn't I bring something to disguise me and keep my ears warm?

The route seems so different to walk it. The houses become more than scenery, and you brush against people's lives as you walk by. I don't want that.

It seems late, in the darkness, in the quiet. Though it cannot be close to twelve, I am desperate to see a clock and reassure myself that I won't miss the bus back. It would be easier to have a car. But the Civic is Mikey's family. The Beast is Mikey's heart. A new car is the future, and I don't have one.

Her car is not in the driveway. I walked half an hour to stand in front of an empty apartment. The downstairs neighbors have their kitchen light on, but the unbroken snow leading to their entrance indicates they are away. I go up the steps on the outside of her house and try the doorknob.

I force my body into the door, and her whole apartment seems to shake. The door has some give, but it's dead-bolted. Her windows are not within reach. She has betrayed me by not being home. To do something, I unscrew the light bulb above her door and throw it into her backyard.

Feeling like something has me treed, I pound down her steps and scamper away from her apartment. Everything around me is more in focus, but I can't think of the name of anything. I long to camouflage myself by running in people's backyard where taller trees demarcate the property lines and create shadows. I could become part of the backyard wildlife that amble around at night, oblivious to what humans are doing. If I could run long enough, my consciousness would dissipate into the air.

I am walking and panting by the time I make it downtown. In the store windows, Christmas trees pass judgment on me. I never imagined that so many brightly colored sentinels could exist in this cold and concrete land. A cousin or a son tree stands to bear witness in the next store.

Janet's salt-covered Firebird is near the entrance of the Whistle Stop Station.

Anger returns to protect and advise me. I walk up to her car to see how it feels to be near it, then allow myself the luxury of continuing through the parking lot. It's packed for a Thursday, but then I realize it is December 23rd and many people have off tomorrow. It's a free day to spend with a hangover. My plan had been to hide in her back seat. But she will not be getting off soon with it so busy.

Despite the realization, I wouldn't even be able to crouch behind the driver's seat, I head back to Janet's Firebird. She is here, and perhaps her shift ends soon. The parking lot is not well-lit, and a conversion van is parked next to her car. This can happen, and I can get away quickly.

My doggedness pays off. Through the glass door at the top of the steps, I see her on one of the bar stools employees sit at when they are off duty. That is why I went to her apartment first. It's her day off.

The first show audience files out the door and drives me from the parking lot. How did I not see this coming? Why did I think there wouldn't be any show tonight as I trekked from her apartment? You can't talk at the bar with someone performing, and her friends would be too busy. Unless she is covering for someone, she shouldn't be here.

There are only six cars left after I walk up and down the street while giving myself a pep talk filled with laughter. The van can still provide cover for me. Though her boss tried to fire her, she is probably helping her friends load up the bus tubs. She's making jokes loudly and not giving me any indication if she will leave in a minute or an hour. This is all one big mess turning into an infliction.

I am halfway across the parking lot and to her car next to the building when one of the cocktail waitresses comes out the door. Janet complained that this person always had an excuse to leave first. I turn right so she cannot see my face.

She's sitting in her car, letting it warm up when I reach the door as if I'm going in. I have to turn around and walk back out of the parking lot like I forgot something.

She does not put the car into gear until I am in the middle of the parking lot's driveway. I move to the side and yell, "It's about time, Bitch" as she passes me. Once her taillights stop bathing me in red, I crouch down in front of the van.

Janet comes down the steps. My legs are hard to move, as if they have been locked in place too long, but I do not have any recollection of time having passed or having any thoughts. My breathing is loud. Is it loud enough that she will hear me? As I move to a squatting position. I see her face and her open jacket. She comes toward me but seems to get smaller. She is slender when I thought she was broad-shouldered. In my head, she had loomed big and powerful. She fumbles with her car keys in the door lock. Her ears have quickly reddened from the cold.

I go to the balls of my feet, ready to free myself from her persecution.

"Janet," a man says, having come out from the bar.

"Hey. Are ya heading home, too?"

"Ya. Do you want me to give you a ride?" He's beside her now. I want to get him, too, for screwing this up. But somehow, I find patience.

"Thanks, but you've had a lot more than me. Maybe you should lie down in the back there for a while." She slaps the van.

"It's too cold to do that alone." His slurring voice sounds familiar.

The whooshing roar of him opening the sliding door to the van startles me. This van is his, but I am not afraid. So I crawl forward and peer at them. While I can't see him at all, Janet is leaning on her car, bent forward at the waist with arms folded. She focuses her eyes on him as if to memorize a sentence written on his face. She has had a lot to drink, too.

"Come on, it will be fun," he says, making me angry.

"Not tonight," she says. "I'm in a bad mood and won't be good company." She puts a cold laugh at the end of her statement.

"Yeah, Minnesota will do that for you," he says, and I realize it's Dave standing there, trying to move in on my girlfriend. "Come on. I'm a nice guy."

Doesn't she know he's playing her? She should have unlocked her car as he stood talking. But instead of moving, she says, "I was just with a comic that said he was a nice guy. I can't handle another nice guy right now." I can't see her mouth move as she says this.

Dave puts his hand on her shoulder, and Janet shrugs it off.

His hands swoop to her arms. He presses his body on hers as he tells her, "Come on. Don't be a tease." With Janet pinned against her car, he reaches for the front of her jeans. I move toward them, but her arms are free, and she shoves him away. He falls back and sprawls out in the van. He scrambles back up and glares at her. But then slams his van door and goes back into the bar.

I am back, hiding in front of the van as she unlocks her car. Her back is to me. The parking lot is empty. And quiet except for the sound of her key missing the lock. For a moment, she stands there, too overcome by crying to get the door open. I have her.

She pulls the door open and slips into the car.

I do not move. She starts the car and guns the engine in neutral a few times. Finally, she puts the car into gear and backs away.

I lash out and punch the front of the van. With my back against the wall, I kick out a headlight and smash the grill. My own limits have trapped me in weakness.

But Mikey is relieved. When she was in danger, I stood up, ready to protect her. Suddenly I'm not hardened, and Dave's life doesn't seem so enviable. She had fear and pain in her eyes when he grabbed her. It was the look I wanted to cause. That I thought I had no choice but to get from her.

But the fear and pain had already been there, too. It was easier not to know that, and it lets her off the hook.

Should it, though? Everyone is tempted to excuse their behavior by what chases them.

I hear a voice in my head. SHE'S NOT THE ONE. But it does not surprise me. SHE HAS DONE NOTHING COMPARED TO WHAT KAREN HAS DONE.

I give the van another kick and head toward the bus station. Yes, I answer. I am still an animal.

42

A parking lot drains from my dream as I open my eyes to the ceiling of my dining room. What happened there is vague, but I don't want revenge anymore. The walk home from the bus station took forever. Was I lost or making sure I wasn't followed?

Have I found a spot in my mind where I am safe?

SOMEONE MUST PAY, the voice from last night says. This voice is instinct. An inborn thought of what to do. IT MUST NOT GO UNPUNISHED. I stare at the smoky, octagon light fixture and wait for messages. Underneath the mattress is the shards of a mirror.

The phone rings and the answering machine records my mother. "Mikey, I've promised not to talk about that awful thing you did in Wisconsin, and you still don't return my phone calls. The girls missed you at Thanksgiving. Please call me back now because I almost had Chet drive up last night." There is a moment of silence. "Call me, Mikey. Goodbye."

For a moment, I picture Chet at my door. He would be hesitating to deliver the message from his wife. I would be wondering why, if she was so worried about her son, she didn't bother to come herself. Then I go over to the machine and erase the message.

I want to replay the voice in my head to determine who it is. If it's God, it is the old-testament God. The cause-and-effect God who kills thine enemies. Is that not an instinct? Someone knocks. "Mikey," Dave calls out.

"Hey," he says when I let him in. "I tried to call you a couple of minutes ago, but your line was busy. I hate to bother you, but could you give me a ride to pick up my car at the shop. Wow. Were you cooking cabbage in here?"

Looking at my apartment through Dave's eyes, I see that the furniture and floor are cluttered with food refuse. My dining room is filled with an un-sheeted mattress. Dirty clothes from the summer take my attention.

My mouth won't move or produce sounds, but I want to ask Dave some things. What happened last night? Is this dirty apartment really mine?

"This is poor timing." Dave shuts the door and takes some hesitant steps toward the couch. "But today is the only day during Christmas break I could get my car in."

"You mean your van. You need a new headlight."

"Mikey, I have the Mazda still. Why would I get a van?"

"You were at Whistle Stop Station."

"Not since summer."

I laugh. "You don't have to lie. I know you were there hitting on my girl last night."

He looks at me. "No. I was taking my mom shopping at the mall."

Dan attacked Janet. Yet I also know he doesn't have a van. He loves his RX-7. "My car got towed away a couple of days ago."

"You better go get it. They charge you daily."

"They can keep it. The person who had it towed can just keep feeling guilty for making them take it." I walk into the dining room and on my mattress and back out into the living room, where Dave is leaning on the arm of the couch.

Dave unzips his jacket. "Mikey, you're not making a lot of sense lately. That's why I'm here. You abandoned all your friends. You hate this new act you're doing, yet it doesn't seem like you think of it as an act."

"Let me ask you something." I sit on the arm of the chair with my feet in the seat. "I know you are the fuck 'em and chuck 'em type. But what do you do when they lead you on, then call it quits? Don't you try to get back at them?"

He scratches his chin like he's figuring out a lie to tell me. "I slept with every woman that gave me the time of day after my divorce. But I was a miserable son-of-a-bitch." I don't want to hear this. He needs to tell me it's right to look out for number one. That it's self-preservation. "I fought her on child support and custody. I picked the fight every time. At one point, I tried to turn the kids against her, but it ate me up. I was depressed, not eating. It gave me anxiety attacks. Finally, I had to forgive her for leaving just to make it easier on me."

SOMEONE MUST PAY. I try to collect myself and hear what he is saying, but that voice in my head is so insistent. "Some things are unforgivable."

"I'm just saying-"

"If anyone would agree with me, I thought it'd be you, Dave. You've been divorced for years, and your whole act is what your wife did to you."

Dave gives me his comic voice. "I-I have some issues. Seriously though, my wife was human and made mistakes like we all do. I let my anger go."

"Did you? You are still trying to fuck every woman to get back at her." If I was a comedian, I might make a joke about saying that to get back at him. "But what you are doing is punishing those other women for her sins."

He looks at me, and I turn away. "I don't know what has you so messed up, Mikey, but you gotta let it go. Listen to me. The only way for things to get better is to let your anger go. Just because I still date a lot of women now doesn't mean I disrespect them anymore. And I'm actually spending Christmas with my ex-wife because both our daughters are home from college, and I am looking forward to it."

"What? What did you say?" SHE IS HOME. I never imagined her being anywhere except at school in Virginia. A problem a thousand miles away. But, of course, she would come home for Christmas. My heart is beating fast as if she was in front of me.

"The girls both made it home this year."

I stand up, breathing hard, rubbing the fingers of each hand together until they form into fists. "Get out," I tell Dave. "Get out. Get out." I grab him. Drag him out of my apartment.

He does not resist other than to scramble to stay on his feet. "Mikey. Hey. Mikey." I give him a shove and shut my door.

SOMEONE MUST PAY.

I put on sweat pants and a pair of jeans. Then I put on three shirts. I find gloves, a hat and put on my jacket and the old work boots from my costume. Think. "Think," I say, pounding my forehead with my fist. "What am I doing? How am I going to do it?" I go to stuff my wallet into my pockets but find it in my hands.

I have one more thing to get, so I open the door to the bedroom. Everything is in its place. The bed is made, and lying on the pillows is the stuffed teddy bear Karen gave me for Valentine's Day. The bassinet is in the corner with folded blankets, and a mobile clamped to it. Next to it is a changing table that matches the crib in my storage unit in the basement. I drop my big jackknife as I pull it out of the nightstand and kneel to pick it up. The stale air reminds me of my grandma's musty church.

Bang. Bang. Bang. "Mikey, let me back in. Let's talk."

DON'T LET HIM DENY YOU THIS.

I do as the voice instructs. STEP ONTO THE BALCONY. SHUT THE DOOR TO HIS POUNDING AND CLIMB OVER THE RAILING. LET YOURSELF FALL TO THE GROUND.

Shock waves roll up my legs, and I fall backward into a snowdrift. I crawl on my hands and feet to the sidewalk.

I'm headed to Vadnais Heights, to Karen's parents' house.

Should I stop myself? Can I walk? Take the bus? I don't want anyone to judge me with their eyes. The solution is in front of me, unable to get into my head.

How bad did I hurt Janet last night? I pinned her against her car. She freed herself, so I smashed the front of her car up.

It is snowing with no wind. The flakes wind down from the black of the already dark sky and into the ceaseless glowing of the city. I sweat in my layers of clothes. The weather and the cold make renting a car a must, but for now, I can use my legs to get to the car rental place on Sixth Street.

Does the rental place close at five? It might already be closed for Christmas Eve. The cars lumbering by with snow piled on their roof and ice packed into the rims tell me it has snowed all day. My tracks are two lines dragged through the unbroken white. At times I tromp through snowbanks, and this makes my feet squish inside my boots.

My legs are heavy as I trudge across the plowed parking lot of National Car Rental. Christ, even if I wouldn't freeze to death, I'd never make it out of Saint Paul.

Inside, the guy asks if I made a reservation. I shake my head. With a sigh, like it will take a long time, he gets my information. He looks at my driver's license and my credit card while I pluck at my clothes to get air into them. After typing into his computer, he slides them back across the counter. He asks if I want insurance. I say no because something will happen, but insurance won't cover it. He makes me sign off on that.

The seat is already as far back as it will go in a blue Ford Taurus, but my head still rubs against the roof. My fingers move with nervous energy, and I have trouble putting the key in the ignition.

With the heat off and the window open, I drive. I get on the freeway and drive behind the drivers going slow to make it to their loved ones safe and sound.

Driving is harder in the suburb. The roads are drifted over, and the curtain of white hides landmarks. Snow crunches under the wheels and explodes as I go through drifts in acts of defiance.

Houses flicker with strands of Christmas lights and glow with green and red floodlights illuminating giant wreaths on their chimneys or sides of houses. The musical stylings of snow blowers echo along the block. Many of the men will be back out in a few hours to clear their territory again. The songs of the snow blowers will be quicker and less labored, and they will hum through the light layer of new snow.

The meandering streets make me crisscross their subdivision several times until I find the house- a large, white, square house with two large bay windows on either side of the main entrance. Her mother's Volvo station wagon sits in front of the garage. They have Christmas lights on the pine tree out front and the shrubbery around the house. A large manager scene recently swept clean reposes on the lawn with a spotlight fighting the snow to illuminate it.

My instincts tell me not to park on their street but in front of a nearby apartment complex with other cheap cars. At first, it's the vague feeling that they have a restraining order against me that makes me take steps to go undetected. The knife I fondle in my pocket reminds me of the real reason.

Without a plan yet, I ask myself some questions. How much did I hurt Janet? Was I practicing for tonight?

THINGS MUST BE SET RIGHT. ATONED.

Out of the car, the cold and darkness force me to only focus on the voice.

My slow approach to the house gives me time to get reacquainted with its big bay window eyes on either side of its dimpled door nose. Red steps are a stuck-out tongue, but it's not a silly home. I crawl through its stately lot with tall trees and look into the eye window of the living room.

They have a large tree that is a blur of green and blinking lights through the wet snow on the window. Christmas presents are piled around it and take up a three feet radius past the skirt. The large stone fireplace warms the empty room.

The room with the second eye window is a sitting room, a den, or whatever you call it. Behind this room is the dining room with the chandelier on. Its glass fixture makes the surrounding room shiny and inviting, like the overhead lights of a gas station on a rainy night.

Going to my knees, I squeeze through their bushes and up to a side window of the sitting room. In the snow and the scratchiness of the tall shrubs, I am a nocturnal animal. No longer human. Almost. Human thoughts still plague me. No, they are not thoughts. They are memories, and I can't get rid of them.

Right now, I only want to survey this lost world.

Her father is sitting in a recliner watching the small TV set. He is tall, balding with a strong face. Mikey sat on that couch and talked to that man. He hoped he would love him as a member of his family, spending holidays and Sunday afternoons in his house, eating with several relatives at the table in the dining room.

Mikey felt normal then, and his uneasiness in this house was only of marrying their daughter and feeling underclass. With Karen to love him, he was good-looking and personable.

Her mother passes in the hall behind and returns to walk into the room and plug in the lights of the Christmas tree. She is a heavyset woman making slow, measured movements to join her husband so they can admire the tree together.

They are so proud of the family portrait they are in. I hate them. They made their daughter, and she made me.

43

Karen spun in her busy days. Mikey waited for her to come around, and he did his best to keep her energized with talk of baby names and wedding plans. Then she slipped away. She canceled plans and left messages with her roommates. As far as he knew, Karen's life kept spinning. He tried to connect and find out what was wrong, but he felt like he was grasping at nothing.

His life became their rare phone calls filled with silence. On his end, he held back words so as not to hurt her. Karen would not tell him why she had nothing to say. So he just showed up at her apartment after the library closed. He had hoped she would be happy to see him. Yet his anger had followed him to the door. Just in case Karen had someone tell him she wasn't home. She fell into his arms. He swung the door shut with his foot, not letting her go.

They moved to the couch while her roommate grabbed something from the kitchen and went to her room to study.

He would have to keep her reassured and prove himself. But at least he had gotten this far. "It won't be easy. We'll have to accomplish the impossible, but we can do it." He waited for her to say something. "Are you all right?"

"Yes. Now."

"We need each other." He planned out what to say next to make sure he should say it. "You can't push me away."

"I could fall asleep with my head on your chest like this."

Mikey laid his hand on her cheek, stroked the softness of her jawline with the back of his fingers. The room darkened with the setting sun. After a while, he thought she had fallen asleep.

"Michael," she said in a distant, tired voice. "I'm sorry for anything I might do."

"Karen."

"And we should wait until after the baby to get married. No one wants to be a fat bride, and I can't deal with planning a wedding now. The minister at the campus church said he will marry us no matter what."

Mike linked his hands together to hold her. "You wanted to get married at your church."

"I can't even think about it right now."

Mike spent the previous two days learning how to sell Filter Queen vacuum cleaners. He had wised up at the end of day two on how they were suckering people needing a job into selling the vacuum cleaners to family and friends. In those two days, he had only learned two things: he didn't want to be a salesman, and you needed to close the deal. "What do you want? A boy or a girl?"

"A boy." She pulled his arm around her waist. "Life is too hard for little girls. Dads always end up disappointed with their daughters, and moms try to toughen them up so they can handle it."

"Kare, we won't be like your parents." He wanted to get her head up and for her to look at him. "Right?"

"Right." She adjusted, so she lay with her back against him. He looked at her roommate's entertainment center. Karen and her roommate had photos of themselves and friends at summer parties. What Mike saw, though, was family pictures of Karen and their kids.

They talked of dance classes and T-ball games. Karen revealed she loved the name Zachary for a boy. Mikey told her he wanted metal trucks for his kid to play with instead of plastic ones. Karen disagreed for safety's sake, but they did not talk about careers or disappointed fathers.

Mikey drove home that night, feeling it had been a beautiful night. But later, when he thought about it too much, he felt tricked.

44

An extra light comes on in the house and makes me crawl through the snow, creep to the edge of the deck, and look through the patio door. I get a glimpse of Karen's face before she is out of view. Then I can only see her torso, a thick, gray sweater floating between the breakfast counter and cabinets. The gray disappears and returns.

I crawl along the deck, my clothes getting wet. Her face should be framed in the window above the sink, but I see the only light fixture. Instead of standing to get a better view, I slink into the snow, not even trusting my instincts now. But even an animal, in a panic, moves only with fear.

The sitting room is empty when I crawl back to it, except for the shining Christmas tree, which is the reason for the open curtains.

Because it is Christmas Eve, Karen must be downstairs with her loved ones eating snacks and opening presents. So I move along the front. I have come here to face her, and that is what I must do. After that, what comes next doesn't matter.

At the edge of the driveway is a Mercury Villager. Who has a minivan?

I run through the yard, falling but not failing (ha-ha) to get to the side window that looks into the living room. The curtains here are shut. What are they trying to do to me? They force me to forearm crawl through the soft, clutching snow to look in the bay window— the eye of the beast.

I have to brace myself, but why?

The window is too big, and I will see too much.

Ahhh. She's there, in the rocking chair, holding a baby and taking its blue snowsuit off. She is talking to him and smiling. I almost pound on the window to get the baby's attention.

But then Karen's sister takes the baby, and I realize he's not Mikey's son.

45

MIKEY'S PAST

Mikey stood at the side of the platform until he got the attention of the performing comedian. The comic was middle-aged with long, black hair. He had a smooth face but creases of loose skin under his chin.

"You have ta understand, I have lived in Minn-a-sota all my life," the comic said. He pointed to a group that told him they were from California. "But I thought I was different. I thought I was sophisticated like you people on the coasts. Well, not you freaks." He laughed with the audience. "But other people on the coasts.

"Then I started to think about it. I related to every St. Olaf story of Rose's on Golden Girls." The audience of fifty or so laughed. "The first time I watched 'Grumpy Old Men,' I thought it was a documentary.

"I also found myself being proud of hearing Minnesota in the national news for like 96 days in a row." He put his hands on his hips. "You know...The coldest spot in the nation today was International Falls."

"I mean, I knew everyone else in Minnesota was a little crazy."

The crowd quickly booed but also laughed. "Well, look atcha selves, eh? I thought I was the one normal person in Minnesota.

"Then one day, I found myself wearing shorts and a parka, and I realized I am one of you people." The crowd applauds. "The name is John Johnson. Thanks, and you guys are my new best friends."

John jogged to the edge of the stage. "Mikey," he said. "You going on?"

"If there's room. I didn't sign up."

"I'll introduce you, then go talk to Brian. It's late, so he won't mind." John stepped back to the mike. "Ladies and gentlemen. It's my pleasure to introduce a regular here at Humphrey's open mike. He is here every Tuesday trying to bum drinks off me. A good friend of mine and of everyone at Humphrey's except the comic he is about to bump- Mikey Haskell."

The audience applauded. Mikey smiled at them as he grabbed the stool from the back of the stage and pulled it up to the microphone. "Well, I've been doing a lot of drinking tonight," he told the crowd. They cheered, and it made him think to start his act out like that every night. "You know that guy that once he gets drunk, just starts talking to you and won't leave you alone? Well, now he has a microphone."

He leaned forward and down to the audience. "And I wasn't even scheduled to perform. I needed someone to talk to, and you people look trustworthy. I've been having problems with my girlfriend, and we had a big fight tonight. We are-"

"How in the hell did you ever get a girlfriend?" a heckler yelled out and got the crowd going.

"Yeah, no kidding," Mikey said. "I'm asking myself the same question. Maybe I shouldn't ever argue with a woman. You know. How many women here would sleep with Brad Pitt?"

All the women in the crowd cheered.

"How about Patrick Swayze?"

The women yelled again.

"Okay. How many women want to sleep with Fred Gwynne?"

One guy yells out, "Yeeeaaahhh."

"Only one woman. You know who I am talking about, right? Fred Gwynne. Herman Munster." Mike imitated Herman Munster. He stomped his feet and waved one finger in the air. "Now, Lily. Ho. Ho. Ho."

"I didn't think any of you would be thinking, 'I gotta get me some of that.' How about Lurch from The Addams Family? No? How about John Goodman, George Wendt, Louie Anderson-" The crowd cheered, but that's because he's from Minnesota. "

"Louie may be the only famous comedian without any groupies. And not just because he's fat. He is also a nice guy, and that's strike two and three on him." The girls laughed, but the guys clapped.

"It's true. A woman will let a good-looking guy sell her car and screw her sister. But a nice guy who treats her right, but got short-changed a dollar ninety-six in the looks, can't get the time of day from her."

The crowd laughed. Mike looked at them glassy-eyed.

"Seriously, though. Women are looking for an excuse to avoid happiness. It scares them. Most of you women avoid it by finding a man who is a jerk, but if you start getting a good thing with a good guy, you find an excuse to end it." Mikey imitated a woman's voice. "Oh, this is feeling too good. I'm too happy. What was I thinking? This guy has a job and morals. I should dump him for that drug dealer that keeps writing me from prison."

Mike returned to his normal voice. "Women think men try to be jerks. You women are right. We try to be the biggest jerks we can because we are trying to impress you.

"Anyway, you all are spinning around me, and I got to pee, so I'm going to let the comic that was actually scheduled to come up now." Mike stumbled across the stage and then let the stage be empty until the next comic could hustle up to the mike. He bolted to the bathroom and threw up. Staggering out, he passed John, who asked him if he was all right. He ignored John, not able to talk.

He got into The Beast and turned the engine over. It cranked until the battery wore down. "Damn it." He leaned back in his seat and watched the windows fog up. Cold seeped into his jacket as he counted the minutes to when the gas flooded into the carburetor would evaporate. Perhaps shortly after, the alcohol and pain would wear off.

She had become untouchable again. Every question about what was wrong, she twisted out without saying anything. In return, she gave him no comfort. He buttressed his promise to be a good husband with apologies, but she was a stone wall tumbling down on him.

"Please, God," he prayed, "Help me. Fix this." Then Mike passed out, sitting in his car.

At three a.m., he snapped awake, his face cold. He turned the ignition without thinking because he was freezing, but the car started. His head pounded, so he closed his eyes to concentrate on hitting the gas when the car sputtered.

A thought stood in his head like a stranger in a trench coat. The thought was how many pregnancies ended in a miscarriage.

Not wanting to, but not able to deny himself from praying it any longer, he said, "God, if you need a baby to go, please take this one."

* * *

Mikey called Karen. That was the only way he found out she had an appointment at a women's clinic. She refused to tell him when. Mikey pictured the procedure being done over and over. His stomach churned, his chest got tight, and his heart-wrung itself every time it pumped blood.

He had prayed for God to take the baby, and then Karen answered his prayer.

46

For a moment, I can't breathe. I fall to my hands and knees and try to take in air. Then I crawl through the snow to the front of the house. My jeans are wet, and my gloves have snow in them. My stomach churns.

YOU KNOW WHAT TO DO.

I crawl on my belly, slithering to the nativity scene in the beam of a spotlight. The animals, Mary, Joseph, and the angel over Him, are about three feet tall, and the baby Jesus is one foot in length. My cold fingers fumble, getting the knife out of my pocket and open. I panic to get it to my wrist.

ATONEMENT.

The knife slices my wrist like a person committing suicide. The blood drizzles onto the baby in the manger. It splatters his face. The sight of blood makes me happy to give an offering to Jesus. I evolved from human to animal. So that the animal could become a sacrifice.

Sins drain from my wrist. "She killed my baby," I tell the angel looking at me with her arms wide open. Then I place Joseph face down on the straw for the shame and shove Mary over with my foot to keep her from doing anything.

My sleeve is warm and wet as I hold it out in front of me. I run through the darkness and the white of the snow until I fall. The world spins as I roll over the snowdrift along the sidewalk. My eyes shut for a moment.

When I open my eyes, my baby is next to me.

I curl up tight next to him. The snow is red. "Why is the snow red?" I ask him, but he is only a baby and doesn't understand the question. He does understand that under this fur and anger is his dad.

My baby is now a girl. I whisper to her, "I prayed for a bad thing, and the next time I saw your mother, you were gone."

It's late at night. Alaine runs off the sidewalk until she is a black form running away from the street light. Mikey chases after her. When he catches up, she is waiting for him on the merry-go-round. She gives it a push and jumps on.

"Mikey." She smiles as she comes around to him. Not because she is happy, but because he needs to know happiness is still possible.

Mikey runs alongside the merry-go-round before jumping on. It is going faster now, and he has to plant his feet wide apart to balance. He closes his eyes and wills the playground to be a time machine and take him back to when he enjoyed this.

The merry-go-round shudders to a stop. He opens his eyes.

"We shouldn't be here," Mikey says.

"I know," Alaine says back. "But I wanted to bring you to the first place I fell in love with you, Mikey. This is where you became part of my family. Father, husband, brother, son."

"Thanks for being with me. I couldn't have been alone tonight." He sits on an intersection of steel bars the kids hang on to.

"Mikey, you'll be okay."

"No. I don't think so."

Alaine comes over and hugs him, standing next to his long, outstretched legs. As they are, she can hold his head level with hers. He buries his eyes on her shoulder.

I turn my head away from this scene and look at my child. "She held me like a baby. Like the way I wish I could hold you." She is wrapped up in blankets so that she is not cold. She is right next to me, but I can't see her face.

Then she is gone.

Oh, God, I want to lie here and die.

Yet, I get up. Karen didn't love me. And even the baby chose to fade away instead of having me as her dad. I experienced love only once. As Alaine held me those few minutes ago.

I flee the house with its window eyes and from the place where I met my baby. God is close by, and I must get away before he answers another prayer. Pain continues to hunt me.

Escape is only delaying being devoured by the pain, but I plunge through the night until my lungs burn. I come to a phone booth. Without any idea of where the rental car is, I call a cab. My blood is on the metal buttons and in pools under the blue shell. I try to stay in the small shelter but stumble and drop to the icy cement.

47

A car with two sets of vertical headlights slogs its way up the street. My vision is blurry from dizziness, but I can tell it's too old to be a taxi. The rutted, sloshy road sends it on a zig-zagging course until it stops in front of me. It's The Beast with a garbage bag duct-taped over the broken window.

An angel appears. Floating above me with wings of light, she lifts me up and puts me in the car.

God doesn't hate me after all.

Next to me, the angel becomes Alaine. I can't say anything to her; I just huddle up to the vent blowing hot air onto the carpet. My face is wet with snow.

"We got to go to a hospital." Alaine looks at my blood-soaked sleeve. I think she is going to touch it, but she throws the car into gear and hits the gas. The tires spin and the car slides sideways until she finally lets up on the accelerator.

Everything fades away from me, and with my eyes closed, I can only try to contemplate why God saved me, but not my baby.

Alaine makes a sudden, sliding stop. In front of us is the entrance to the emergency room. "How did you know where to find me?" I mumble with my eyes still closed. It was good to see my baby, even better than the knife across my wrist.

She puts her hand to my face for a moment. "Please stay awake," she says. I do my best to open my eyes. "You called me. I think you were trying to call a taxi company. Something was wrong. You barely got your words out, but I couldn't call the cops. So I came."

"Why?"

She gets out and opens my door so that the cold air hits me. "Can you walk?"

I struggle to get up. "Why did you come?" I'm frantic for her to answer my question.

"Because maybe someday you will make a joke out of it. Maybe you'll say, 'You don't have to pay cab fare if the cabby picks you up in your own car.'" She grabs me when I falter. We get me to stand up. My angel is crying. "Do you think you'll ever say that?"

We take several steps onto the sidewalk. Alaine struggles to keep me up. I see the doors of the emergency room. Then I see the sidewalk as I fall to it.

48

A fluorescent light flickers above me. The bed I am on is narrow and firm. Noises from outside the door tell me I'm in a hospital. All night long, I heard carts being pushed down a hallway and people talking, but everything seemed to take place far away.

Alaine has said something to me, so I look at her for a moment without meeting her gaze. Then my eyes flit around the room, which tries to be comforting and friendly, but has too many blank surfaces.

"You sure seem surprised to see me," she says.

I struggle to get up. My limbs are too weak to support me, but my sudden movement brings a person in scrubs from the corner of my room to the foot of my bed.

Alaine is looking at me with her jaw set, but I want to know where I am. Why am I here? Why is Alaine here? My heart races, and my palms get sweaty by having her near.

I scratch the bandage on my left wrist, and she backs away, startled. Why shouldn't she be afraid of me, I think, but when she sees what I am doing, she comes closer again. She has not left me. Talk to me. I want to plead this to her, but the words won't come out.

Perhaps it's because she is already asking me a question, and I need all my concentration to understand anyone.

She takes my hand as she waits for my answer to her question, but I can only try to convey how thankful I am with my eyes.

Dan comes in, and we both look at him. As he stops to survey the room, the medical person touches Dan's arm and says something before slipping out the door.

"Are you this stupid?" he asks. His voice is in my ear. "Are you a glutton for punishment?"

"He slashed his wrist."

"Did you want him to take you with him?"

"When he called me, he wasn't making sense," she says. Her voice is still far away. With almost detached curiosity, I want to find out what she means. "He said he needed a taxi right away and gave the corner he was on. I was afraid no one else could find him."

"What's the matter with you? Even taking his old jalopy on the road was dangerous."

"I wanted him to see I could never impound it. That he used to trust me enough to have a key for it. And he was in Karen's neighborhood. I was worried about her safety, too."

What is she talking about? I can't quite remember what happened, but I know I've done something.

The nurse knocks and comes in. She introduces herself and tells me she needs to get my vitals. This woman in burgundy scrubs asks me questions, but I can't answer her. My speech is gone because my transformation is complete. But why am I here and not free and wild and alone? Or in a zoo? Or dead?

The burgundy woman stops asking me questions and comes at me with something to put around my upper arm.

My instinct tells me it is a collar that injects poison, so I grab it when she gets near me. This person is trying to kill me, so I push her away. People come running and hold me down on the bed.

I struggle. They turn me on my side. After that, nothing.

For the longest time, God stands at the foot of my bed. I know this though I can't focus my eyes. For hours, I blink. Finally, my vision sharpens to find Chet and Mom next to me. I turn my head away.

Later, I wake up. My muscles are unmovable. Janet, Alaine, and Karen are in the room and come toward me. My vision is fuzzy again, and I can't tell who is who. The closest one says, "Mike, I am your nurse. The doctor started you on Haloperidol." Why would she say that to me? I am too tired to find out.

The lights are down low, and yet my vision is blurry. So is my thinking. I want to fall back asleep to get away from my frustration with this, but I have to pee. As soon as I stand, a nurse comes into my room. She knows what I need and guides me to the bathroom. She turns me around, so I sit down. Exhaustion leads me into sleep on the toilet, but the nurse urges me back to bed.

My child is dying. That is where I live. I am shattered, and everything that made me happy is gone.

A thought bursts through the anguished mist. It's the realization I didn't hurt Janet. I am crouched behind a van, ready. Perhaps it's only that I see she lives in a similar place- alone and not knowing which way to turn- but it's important that I stopped myself.

Now in the red snow, I see my baby. He is beautiful, and I love him, but he leaves me.

I cannot go back to the pain. But my child and her mother existed, and there's no going on with pretending they did not.

It is less of a struggle to open my eyes, but I still can't see very well, and my limbs are still stiff. Mom has been in and out of the room.

Alaine is here now. She is reaching toward me. Her hands caress my cheeks. She wipes something away with her thumb. Am I crying? All I did to her and all she knows I have done. She still came for me.

Dan's voice comes from behind her. "What's the matter with him, Lainey? Can't he talk?"

"I don't know. He hasn't said anything." Her voice is unsteady. "I should have been there for Mikey when it happened." She's talking to Dan but looking at me. "I tried to keep his mind off it, but I didn't really try to help him. I didn't really talk to him."

She didn't know what to do. I can finally think that. It allows what I thought she was doing to get reconciled with who she is. "You were there last night," I tell her. Her hand goes to her mouth. "We sat together on a merry-go-round."

She shakes her head.

My throat is so dry I can barely get my words out. "Yes. We went round and round, and you let me talk."

"That wasn't last night, Mikey. That was months ago. You've been in the hospital for the last three days."

"You have to understand that at first, I couldn't see my baby. I hoped it wasn't true, then I prayed she would miscarry. I made it happen." My chest heaves as the grief comes. "But then I began to picture her as a baby girl. Karen and I would end up fighting with her as a teenager, and I practiced what to say to make sure we made up. I could feel her arm in mine at her wedding. I fell in love with the baby, and I thought Karen loved me. But it was too late."

Dan steps to Alaine as her hand wipes more tears from my face. Alaine says, "It was hard for her. She thought it was the best thing for everybody."

"I had already prayed for the baby to stop existing. I killed the baby, not her. She only realized that I was so repulsive that she couldn't love me." Alaine leans over and hugs me. I cling to her and hug her.

"Don't say that," she says in my ear. "She panicked. You didn't know a lot of things about her. She's still having problems."

"Then I fell in love with you. It sounds sick and twisted, I know, but I did." She is still hugging me, her face beside mine, so I don't have to see her reaction. "Loving you was supposed to be my salvation."

"Mikey, you are my best friend."

"I know," I say. "I know you are not in love with me. That made me want to hurt you." It was foolish to try for her love. It was why I never did until I was desperate. Someone like her would not pick someone like me. "You were just so good to me."

"That's because I do love you. How long have you felt this way?"

A doctor knocks and comes in. She introduces herself and says, "Someone's talking now. That is good news. Now I can ask you some questions if you two will step out of the room."

"Now?" Alaine asks her.

Dan says, "I thought it was a good idea to tell the nurses, but then they wouldn't wait."

Alaine gathers up her purse and coat, and Dan comes to stand next to her. "I'll be back later, Mikey." She gives me a small smile. It is everything. "Okay?"

EPILOGUE

The house is empty, but I am not alone. Tammy and Carrie are sharing a room so that I have my old bedroom. In the quiet of the afternoon, I am writing Alaine a letter.

With the beard gone, the space between my nose and upper lip looks enormous. The shave and haircut seem melodramatic, and I still crave the animal's unfeeling. This is hard. But it has been easier with your letters and visits. I appreciated what you said in your last letter. Appreciated? The word sounds phony, but I needed to hear what you said about love.

I stop and pick up her letter to reread this part to make sure I got it right. I do that a lot lately, and my therapist says I need to start trusting myself, but I just want to be sure that what I say and do is based on reality.

Don't be embarrassed. I think love is there to get twisted into the boundaries you set for it. It is there to be shaped into what you need. I love Dan, and I twisted that love into marriage because that is what I needed. I love you, but I needed you to be a friend, so I twisted love into a friendship. When you lost Karen, you needed someone to replace her. *You took our friendship love and twisted it to romantic love because that is what you needed, and it is the same energy.*

I pick up my pencil. Later, on the phone in my parent's kitchen with my sisters running in and out, I'll make the joke to Alaine that it sounds like she is making balloon animals out of love. But for now, I am thankful that having one phone in the house and Chet not wanting a big phone bill is forcing me to write to Alaine. I can write it down, get it out without making a joke.

And I agree. I think people have feelings for others, and you assign those feelings a label according to what you need or what society dictates. I'll take your love in the form of friendship. Now that I am thinking straight again, I can give you friendship love. That you still want it shows how amazing you truly are.

Chet got me a job, and I am moving to an apartment here in Duluth at the end of the month. I am still unsure if I can go back to doing stand-up. I feel good, though. Janet and Karen's parents replied to my apology letters. The letter to Karen is too hard to do right now. If that fetus had a soul, it slipped away and found life somewhere good, but I still wish I would have done something differently. But if you can forgive me for all I have done, then I can forgive myself. I can grieve for my baby. I can wish Karen happiness. I can move on.

Love (in every sane way possible),

Mikey

The winter air on my freshly shaven face is immediate and icy. It is snowing, but not cold as I walk to drop Alaine's letter in a letterbox. I do not hurry in this task.

The End

ACKNOWLEDGMENTS

I would also like to thank the writing community of Oshkosh. The Likely Writers Conference, The Oshkosh Area Writers Club, and The Carmel Crisp Writers for teaching and inspiring me. Special thanks to Ruth Percey, who created this community I love, and to Dixie Jarchow, who is my partner on our show The Author Showcase and my partner in crime.

ABOUT THE AUTHOR

Thomas Cannon was raised on a small dairy farm near Spencer, Wisconsin. While drawn to the honest work of farming, he followed a passion for writing and graduated with a bachelor's degree in English from the University of Wisconsin- Stevens Point. In August 2021, he was named the Poet Laureate of Oshkosh. Author of many short stories and poems, he is dedicated to growing his local writing community. Each year he helps to organize the Lakefly Writers Conference and co-hosts Author Showcase on the Oshkosh Media Channel. He and his wife have raised three children and have two grandchildren.

www.ingramcontent.com/pod-product-compliance
Lightning Source LLC
Chambersburg PA
CBHW060437180626
46817CB00007B/2853